HER ROCK

CENTER CITY FIRST RESPONDERS

REINA TORRES

Copyright © 2020 by Reina Torres

All rights reserved.

This book is a work of fiction. Names, characters, places, and incidents are the products of this author's imagination or used fictitiously. Any resemblance to actual events or locales or persons living or deceased is entirely coincidental.

Copyright 2020 by Reina Torres

No part of this work may be used, stored, reproduced, transmitted without the express and written permission from the publisher, except for brief quotations for review purposes, as permitted by law.

Model Photo Credit: Golden Czermak - Furious Fotog

Model Credit: Lovett Taylor

CENTER CITY FIRST RESPONDERS

If there's someone in pain or in need in Center City, these courageous men and women are there to help. Fire, Police, Medical and Dispatch: they'll be there.

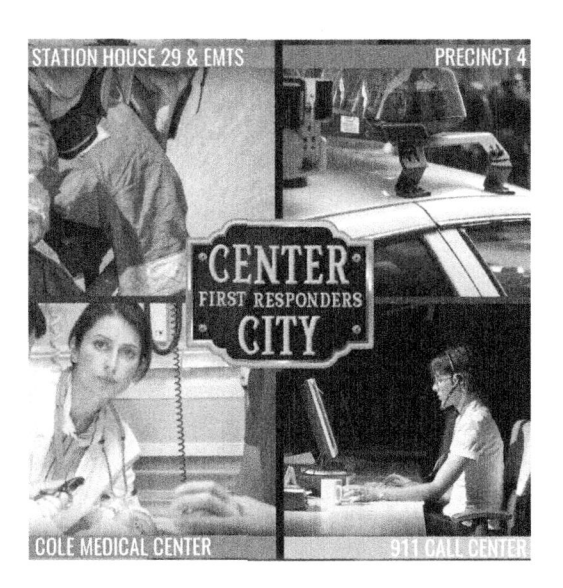

WILD HEARTS

Dr. Roan Ashley & Pilar Bravo

Pilar Bravo moved from San Antonio to Center City not just for the job, but because she needed a new start. Including, time away from her huge and over attentive family. In Center City she could focus on her job as a Police Officer and live her own life. She wasn't expecting to find anyone who could handle a woman who didn't need a man to protect her. She could do a fine job on her own.

Roan Ashley is the top ER Trauma Doctor at Cole Medical. He's not just cool under pressure, he's an iceberg. That all goes out the window when he sees CCPD Officer Pilar Bravo injured during the apprehension of a robbery suspect. It doesn't stop there. While they begin to know each other off the clock, she keeps coming into the ER for injuries on the job.

He's falling fast for Pilar, but it seems like everywhere she goes, danger follows and while his calling is to heal people, to treat their wounds, the idea that she could be taken from him at any moment makes him question if he's the right person for her.

Being a female officer adds layers of stress onto an already stressful job. Equality is a great idea, but not everyone subscribes to that ideal. Pilar struggles with the difference between experience and seniority, and personal clashes lead to a dangerous showdown on patrol.

Roan is left to struggle with his own fear of losing someone he loves and lending his strength when he can't use his medical skills to save her. Standing on the side of the fight is not something he's used to, but he'll do what he needs to do... for her.

Discover the interwoven lives of first responders in Center City. When there's trouble, the brave and devoted members of Center City's Fire, Medical, & Law Enforcement entities band together to make their home a better place, falling in love along the way.

Start your Wild Heart racing!

HER ROCK

Martin "Rock" Ferris & Kate Turner

A Sergeant in the CCPD, Kate Turner has always known what she wanted to do with her life. She wasn't the kind of person who could sew up a wound or deliver a baby... okay, she'd done that once, back when she was on patrol, but now her job was watching out for her people and making them better officers. Who was watching out for her? She didn't need someone to do that, thank you very much!

Martin "Rock" Ferris was a man who would walk through fire for his friends and did so on a regular basis as a member of the Rescue Crew from House 29. As broad in the shoulder as he was brave, he never left anyone behind and he was always there to lend a hand in the thick of a crisis. The problem in his life was that the very person he wanted to protect more than anyone else didn't want him around on a regular basis.

It wasn't that they weren't compatible. They knew how to get along fine enough when they had their hands on each other and their clothes off. And while Kate used her sharp tongue to tell him exactly where to step off, she also knew exactly how to drive him wild. And when she let him, he returned the favor over and over again.

But that's all she'll give him. Those stolen moments in the dark. Kate doesn't want to let him into her heart. Men don't stick around for long and she'll never give Rock the chance to break her heart into a thousand pieces. When her world is upside down and everything is falling down around her ears, she knows her family is there for her, but she'll never let them see the abject fear and deadly doubt that's creeping into her mind. She hides that away and puts on a brave face.

Martin is determined to tear down her walls because he knows that he's ready to stand there between her and danger. He'll always be Her Rock.

ROCK & KATE

PROLOGUE

The first time Martin saw Kate Turner she was squaring off against a guy who was half a foot taller than she was with maybe thirty or forty pounds more on his frame. Oh, he'd never tell her the weight part. He was a guy who'd lived long enough to know when to shut up.

Mostly.

Heading back to his apartment, he'd slowed behind a couple of cars rubber necking at something on the other side of the road.

A fender bender. And a man who looked like he was a few choice words away from a physical throw down.

The woman he was towering over didn't look the least bit intimidated by his size or the red flush on his face.

When he lunged at her, Martin had all but jumped out of his truck.

She shoved the man back and, for a moment, the man in the middle of his burst of road rage managed to step back and out of the range of her hands.

Martin pulled off to the side of the road and left his car at the curb.

By the time he wound his way through the milling traffic, he saw the man put a meaty hand on her shoulder.

He'd broken into a run, ready to separate the man's head from his neck.

And he'd come up short.

Before he could do anything to help, the woman had the enraged man on his knees, his arm bent up behind him.

That's when Martin slowed his steps, coming into her line of sight.

She held out her free hand to him.

"Stop!"

Holding his hands up in surrender, he came to a halt in the street.

"Who are you? Why are you here?"

"I'm Martin Ferris from Firehouse Twenty-Nine. I came to help you, but I guess you don't need it."

The smile that touched her lips was sweet, maybe even a little rueful. "Yeah, I think I'm good."

Reaching around behind her, she moved her coat out of the way and pulled a pair of handcuffs from her back pocket and that quick flash of movement also showed the badge she had clipped to her waistband at her side.

"Just don't get run over standing there, Martin. I've got my hands full with this asshole."

As he watched, she cuffed the man and phoned in a call to the station asking for transport.

When that was done, she gave him a curious look. "What are you waiting for?"

He'd smiled, feeling a little like a hormonal teenager talking to the hottest girl in school. "If I said I was waiting around to make sure he doesn't give you trouble, it wouldn't be a lie. But more than that, I'm waiting for an introduction. You know who I am, but I don't know-"

"Kate Turner."

Kate. The name was burned into his memory. The way she said it, the proud look in her eyes, and the stubborn lift of her chin.

"Sergeant Kate Turner, CCPD."

Damn. An officer with a pair of cuffs and body that could make him hard in a heartbeat? Fuck him.

He was in love. Heaven help him.

[1]

ROCK & KATE

Her alarm went off like clockwork. And since that was its job, she didn't pick it up and throw it across the room.

Normally, she'd give it a good open-handed smack and roll out of bed and into the shower.

Normally.

But not this morning.

No, this morning was different. She felt the mattress sink behind her and before she could make a grab for the edge of the bed, he had a hold of her.

Martin Ferris. Resident silver fox of Firehouse Twenty-Nine. They called him Rock and there was one major reason she agreed with them.

He wrapped his arm around her body and dragged her back against his larger frame. And she felt it pressed up against her.

Before she could muster up a snarky comment, he had his hand on her breast, his fingers working magic on her bare flesh.

When he'd shown up the night before, just before

midnight, she couldn't send him back home. Not with that haunted look on his face. Another firefighter assigned to the same Rescue Crew had been injured while trying to free a woman from her wrecked car.

From what she'd heard through the Center City grapevine, it had been a mess. The result of a chain reaction accident involving no less than seven cars. Snow and ice were always a danger, but Center City snow and ice in the winter were deadly.

She'd seen her own share as a police officer, but she wasn't the one to climb into a wreck to save someone.

Sure, she had some emergency medical training, but not enough to do what Rock and his crew did on a regular basis.

And the look on his face when she'd opened her door spoke volumes. He'd been wrecked, turned inside out.

"How much time do you have before you have to get out of bed?"

She hummed as if considering the notion.

Kate didn't want to tell him the truth, because if he knew they had almost an hour before she had to be awake and moving, she would really be late, because Rock could take an hour and then keep her in bed all day long.

It wasn't just his cock… he knew how to use his hands and his mouth… just thinking about how he liked to feast on her had her dripping wet.

Rock slipped his leg between hers and growled into her ear. "Looks like you're awake… all over."

As if to prove his point, his palm skirted over her nipple and she hissed out a curse as it tightened into a point.

"You feel so damn good, baby."

Her teeth ground together. "No 'baby' talk."

His teeth closed over her earlobe, making her wince at the sudden pressure. "Whatever you say, *Katie*."

Frustrated in so many ways, she arched back against him and heard him groan. She didn't even bother to hide her satisfied snort of laughter.

Then his hands were on her. One roughly pulling at her breast, the other tunneling under her prone form, past her hip, so he could slip his fingers between her legs and stir her even more.

She bucked against his hand as his fingers expertly massaged her clit.

Damn, why did it have to be so good with him?

She shoved that disturbing question into the back of her head and tried to hold back her building orgasm. She wanted more first. She wanted him, first.

Kate reached back a hand and grabbed at him, finding his hip and then his thigh. She dug her fingers into the thick, corded muscle of his leg as he found a particularly good angle on her clit.

"Fuck!"

"Is that what you want, Katie? You want me to fuck you?"

She managed a half-groan, half-moan as she rolled forward, bringing him with her.

His hand left her breast and instead of her instinctual need to grab his hand and pull it back, she gripped the edge of the bed and arched her back, pressing against him.

"Damn it," he groaned, deepening his voice straight into an intimate growl. "You know I love your ass."

She was hoping he wasn't going to get talkative, that's not what she needed.

Then he was against her back, his hand hooking under her thigh to lift it and make enough space between her legs for his larger body.

The way his cock pushed inside of her always gave her a

thrill, sending shivers up her spine. At first it was just the blunt tip pushing in until her folds wrapped around him and pulled him inside.

Rock pushed deeper, sinking into her body with a loud, aching groan. "Dammit, Katie. I fucking love the way you feel around me."

Oh, she loved it too.

Needed it like the air she breathed sometimes, the rest of the time-

She pushed the thoughts away when he pulled back and nearly slipped free, ready to reach for him.

Then he was there again, ending his long, bone-jarring thrust with a hitch of his hips.

"Yes." She'd almost added a 'please' after the word. "Yes, like that."

"Fuck, yeah, Katie. Just like that."

He thrust in again, ending with a grunt, punctuating the stroke that buried him inside of her.

Kate was losing her mind as he pumped into her body. Having his weight on top of her and his cock filling her from behind, she was tempted to call in sick and let him love her all day long.

"Tell me how close you are, Kate. Tell me what I need to do to get you off because I'm getting close. So damn close."

Over and over, he pounded into her and she was almost sure that they'd end up on the floor if they continued on for much longer.

"Kate-"

She heard the way he ground out her name between his teeth and knew she wouldn't last longer than he did, not if he came inside of her.

"Do it, Rock." She gasped as his hips picked up speed. "Take me with you."

"Anything, Katie. Any. Thing. For. You."

Oh god.

She felt him twitch inside of her and a moment later her heat mingled with his release.

It was that feeling, the rush of energy moving from him and into her that tossed her into the storm.

She came down slowly, heaving breath after breath from her lungs as she fought for control. The fight wore her out and the warmth of his laughter reached her ears.

"Babe-"

"I told you," she turned her chin toward her shoulder, "no baby talk."

Suddenly the sound of her alarm cut through the relative silence of her apartment.

"Kate, I-"

"Shit. I've got to get in the shower."

He'd barely pulled out of her body when she swung her legs over the side of the bed and got to her feet.

"Kate."

She grabbed the outfit that she'd set aside for work and turned to look at him from the doorway to her bathroom.

He sat up and she tried to ignore the fact that he was naked and still half hard as he looked up at her.

"I wanted to know if you'd come with me to Ciro's tonight. We're doing a fundraiser to help with some of Seth's upcoming medical bills."

She balked at the idea for a number of reasons, but it was his next few words that had her shifting uncomfortably away from him.

"Then, maybe you can come back to my place for the

night. I start my next twenty-four tomorrow morning, but we would have the whole night-"

"We have an agreement." She heard the edge in her voice, and she saw the troubling crease between his brows, but she had to draw the line. "This," she made a vague gesture between them, "isn't a relationship. You know that."

There was a bitter taste on her tongue, but then again, maybe it was just morning breath.

"Look, you're welcome to stay as long as you want. I have to get going into work. If you want, I'll check in with the officers who're doing the accident investigation and get you whatever information they have."

With that, she turned and walked into the bathroom, partially closing the sliding antique door behind her.

The shower was hot, steaming up the room in moments. When Kate stepped under the spray she hissed out in pain, but it was no less than she deserved. She felt like an ass for what she'd said to Rock. She could have been easier on him. After the night before when she'd let him in, worried about how he was faring, it had only been too easy to take him in her arms because she knew exactly how perfectly they fit together.

That didn't mean that they were meant to be together. Her brother Roan had broached the subject a few times. She didn't blame him, not really. He'd fallen hard and fast for Pilar. They'd clicked from day one. What they had was... different.

She had an understanding with Rock. They had crazy chemistry from the get-go, but that's all it was. The time they spent together wasn't about hearts and flowers. They scratched an itch for each other. They took the edge off. And they did it so damn well.

That's why she had to draw the line.

No one had ever known her body the way Rock did. The way he could arouse her. The way he knew exactly what she needed. Hard. Fast. Slow. Sensual. He knew it and he did it for her just like she did it for him. It was hot and instinctual between them. Emotions... well, they didn't factor in. It was better that way. Clean. Simple.

Everything she needed without the emotional push and pull.

Fuck, she didn't have time for that in her life.

Keeping her officers in line and living took up every spare moment. Getting fucked by Rock kept her sane and really, no one wanted to see what she was like when she was tied up in knots.

No. One.

She grabbed the scratchy bath towel that she'd picked up at a Chinatown street fair from the hook on the wall and scrubbed away all of the troubling thoughts that Rock had stirred up. When she got out, she wrapped her towel around her body and slid the hanging door open.

"Rock, I-"

The bed was empty and given the silence of the apartment she knew that he was already gone.

Great.

No, really.

That's what she wanted.

It was easier like this.

Kate dropped her towel and reached for her camisole. She pulled it on and got dressed quickly. If she hurried up, she could get a breakfast burrito from Peggy Ann's Diner on the way to work.

She could even get extra cheese. With all of the exercise she'd had the night before, it wasn't going to hurt.

Then why did it feel like she was already hurting?

. . .

Precinct Four was buzzing a little more than usual when Kate arrived. Her brother Walker came up to her first as she hung up her jacket and dropped her keys into the top drawer of her desk.

"What have you heard?" He sat down on the edge of her desk, stretching his legs out.

Kate took a moment before she answered knowing that what she'd heard had all been from Rock.

And if she said that, Walker would fixate on that and she just didn't want to talk about it. The odd exchange that Rock and she had had a little over an hour before was still bothering her.

This, she reminded herself, was the reason why she didn't do relationships.

"Kate?"

She turned to look at Walker and saw a little impatience in his expression. He was different from his brother... *their* brother in so many ways, even if they would look like clones if they tried. Yet, Roan would give her a hug and talk to her later. Walker? Well.

"Do you have news or not?"

"Look, Walker, I just got in. What do you know?"

He huffed out a sigh. "Only what Jerk-zek deigned to tell me while he poured out the last of the coffee and left the empty on the heater."

She winced at the image that put in her head. "Full of himself?"

"When isn't he?"

That was the question, wasn't it? Detective Henry Jerzek certainly had an attitude, but his skills as a detective were usually top-notch. He was just a special kind of asshole. Not exactly the perfect example of an officer from the CCPD, but he did manage to close his cases.

"I'll talk with him in a bit. I have to talk to the Captain first. Get the assignments for my people." She started to walk away but caught sight of Walker smiling at her.

That was never good.

She turned back. "What?"

Walker sat up a little taller on her desk and tried to school his smile. It didn't work, but she gave him points for trying.

"Why are you smiling at me?"

He shrugged. "You're such a mama bear. '*My people*.'"

She rolled her eyes. "It's a thing. I'm responsible for them. They're my subordinates, not my children."

"I guess," he bit the inside of his cheek, "especially since one of your 'people' is going to be your sister-in-law soon."

"Our sister-in-law," she reminded him. "You're going to stand up for Roan, remember that. So, don't be a dick to his fiancé."

"Dick?" He scoffed. "Watch that potty mouth here in the precinct, hmm?"

Looking around, she realized that no one's eyes were watching, and she knew where the security cameras were, so she flipped him off. "You can get your," she mouthed A S S, "off my desk. I've got work to do."

She went straight to the Captain's office, but he was on the phone, so she stood just outside of the door thinking. Ruminating. It wasn't helpful.

Family. Relationships. Yuck.

Yes, their brother Roan was going to marry one of her officers. Pilar Bravo was a recent transplant from San Antonio Texas and just happened to hit it off with her brother on one of Pilar's many visits to the Cole Medical Center Emergency Room.

Pilar was an excellent police officer. She had law enforcement in her blood. Her elder brother was a Special Agent in the FBI back in Texas, but where most of Kate's officers were male, Pilar was female and also on the petite side. Kate was only a few inches taller than her, but she understood what it was like to have people try to push her around because of her height and her gender.

Pilar's visits to the ER were troubling, but she handled herself well when confronted and she'd earned a lot of respect from her fellow officers when she'd been injured in the line of duty protecting another officer who had caused her nothing but trouble.

"Hey." Pilar stepped up beside her and Kate couldn't help but smile. Pilar's energy and devotion were always the best parts of Kate's workday. "I thought I'd catch you on the way to work, maybe carpool."

Kate didn't know what to say.

"I mean, it's okay if you were busy." Pilar's smile brightened. "I thought I saw Rock's truck outside on the curb last night when Roan and I ran out for some Cherry Limeades from SONIC. I'm totally addicted to those things. Roan said it's been a while since he's seen Rock's truck out there. You know he can park it closer, right? We have plenty of room along the curb."

There really wasn't much she could say to that. She certainly wasn't going to get into the specifics of her non-relationship with Rock standing in the precinct.

"Yeah." She had to shuffle her thoughts around to put something out there. "I'll let him know, but Rock does what Rock does. I don't have much I can say to influence him about anything."

Pilar's smile faltered a little, and her gaze slid to the side. Kate knew that was Pilar's 'putting the puzzle together' expression. And she was too damn good at it for Kate's peace of mind.

"Have you put any thought into when you and Roan can take a trip down south to see our father and Cora?"

Pilar beat a quick retreat like Kate had expected her to. As big and wonderful of a family as Pilar had back in San Antonio, she was more than a little nervous about meeting Roan's mother. Maybe it was a little bit of desperation that made Kate ask the question, but as much as she loved her brothers and she really did care for Pilar, it wasn't easy to have reminders that the kind of relationship that Pilar had was one Kate couldn't see having for herself.

The Ashleys lost their father when he passed on, but Kate's dad had left her mom for another woman. He'd married her and a few years later, he'd left her behind too. For years, Kate's father had told her that she was the only woman who could stand him, and he was likely to die a bachelor. That lasted until he met Cora Ashley. When she finally met Cora, Kate had to admit that she was an amazing woman, Kate just didn't believe her dad was in it for Happy Ever After.

And it just made it hard for her to see the same for herself.

It was easier for her to see it for Pilar and Roan. They both had great examples of loyal, dedicated families.

Yes, that made her cynical. But cynical, in her head, meant smart. You don't get your heart destroyed if you don't give in. That was her mantra. That was her decision.

It's just that she was beginning to see that Martin wasn't going to abide by the ground rules they set up. Not for much longer. He wanted more time with her. Wanted her to go over to his place for a night here and there.

It was tempting. She'd been curious about what his 'space' looked like. The man cave for the caveman that she knew and lo- liked a lot.

But that was a line she wasn't going to cross. Not yet.

Likely never.

The Captain dropped his phone on his desk and got up, reminding her why he'd busted the screen on a half dozen phones since she'd known him.

"Well, that was a waste of time. Turner? You wanted something? My left nut, perhaps? It seems like the Chief already has the other one in a vice."

Oh great, talking about balls before shift change. It was going to be a kick ass day! "Just wanted the assignments for today, sir."

Shrugging, the captain reached over to the pile on the corner of his desk. "Here. This will give you an idea of the crap that came down over night. We're not anticipating a lot of carryover from that to your shift, Turner, but forewarned and forearmed and all that bullshit."

"Yes, sir. I'll meet with my officers and get them out on the street."

"Such a good little sergeant, hmm? Getting right down to work." The smirk on his face was a call back to another era of policing. Another era of Center City. He wore a strong aftershave. His hair held a bit too much product to look natural. Captain Catalano also seemed to wear suits from a past decade… or two. There were times just like that very moment when she felt like he was measuring her up as an officer and found her wanting because she didn't have the same balls that he seemed to bring up more often than he should.

"Thank you, sir. I believe that's exactly what I am."

She walked away with the folder in her hand, her back ramrod straight. She loved her job. She loved serving the people of Center City. And she loved most of her officers but dealing with men like the Captain really put a damper on her mood.

And reminded her that there were good men out there too.

She just couldn't let herself depend on it being for the long term.

So, she just focused on the here and now. She came to a stop in the middle of the bullpen. "Okay, folks, gather up. We've got our marching orders. Let's get to it."

[2]

ROCK & KATE

Ciro's Bar was hopping when Rock got there that evening. There wasn't an empty bar stool or table that he could see, but it didn't matter, he didn't have to stay long. He came to drop off a bunch of cash for Seth and put in an appearance, so he didn't take any crap on his next shift.

It wasn't that he didn't want to spend time with his friends and other firefighters in the area. He had no problem with that. He just wasn't quite in the party mood.

That was entirely on him.

As he waited in turn to get to the front of the line at the bar to press his money into the bunker boot at the corner of the bar, he let his gaze roam over the room to see who he could recognize.

Some firefighters from nearby houses were easy to recognize and a few from farther flung stations had showed. Some who didn't usually venture away from Smokey Joe's Bar, another firefighter haunt, were there too.

Even with all of the familiar faces in the crowd, Rock made it all the way up to the bar before he spoke.

"Patrick, good to see you tonight."

Patrick McGillis, the manager of Ciro's bar, gave him a nod. "You too, Rock. Kind of expected to see you last night. Were you at the hospital all night?"

"No, I had some- somewhere to be." He could hear the dark edge in his own voice. He needed to pull it together. "I went back this afternoon. But Seth was out cold with the meds after another surgery. Still, the nurses say he's doing good. Better than they expected." He stuffed a roll of cash into the boot on the counter and put a twenty on the well-varnished bar top. "Whiskey, neat."

Patrick nodded again, but his mouth had a thoughtful twist to it. "You okay, Rock?"

He bent to pick up a bottle from under the counter and when he stood back up, Rock had eased the tension in his face. He hoped that was enough to avoid more probing questions from the Manager.

"One foot in front of the other like everyone else, Patrick." He watched as the other man poured a healthy dose of whiskey into the glass. "Damn glad we're holding a fundraiser-"

"Instead of a wake." Patrick sighed and nudged the glass toward Rock. "The crew from Twenty-Nine is in the back. They'll find you a seat."

Rock picked up the glass and walked away from the bar. He knew Patrick would have continued to wheedle him for more information. But another customer stepped up to the bar and that gave Rock the chance to walk away.

The instinct to toss the contents of the glass back in one gulp weighed heavily on him, but he only took a sip as he worked his way back through the crowd and under the seemingly never-ending sea of Christmas lights dangling from the ceiling.

Voices called out to him and he answered with a nod or chin lift, trying to put in enough of a smile that they couldn't see the dark mood that he was fighting off.

It wasn't Kate's fault, he reasoned. They'd made their wants clear from the start. It had started one night a little over a year before.

He'd moved into an interim apartment while construction on the Brickhouse Lofts was finishing up. Unexpected delays in construction had left him without a place to stay and he'd heard of a temporary vacancy on Brewery Road. It wasn't really named that on street signs, but it's what locals called it, like people called Las Vegas Boulevard, the Strip.

Buildings which had constituted the center of alcohol production in Center City in the late 1800s and into the earlier part of the 1900s, had been retooled as clothing factories around the advent of Prohibition, and had gone on to other trades and manufacturing, but in the year 2000 it became the "in" place to live.

For Rock, it was just a temporary rest stop as he'd given up his apartment to live in the Lofts.

Seeing the smiles and hopeful looks of his friends, Rock decided that he needed some time to think, and passed through the back door leading to the outdoor patio. It was crazy cold out there but that's what he was counting on. He wanted privacy.

Leaning against the back wall, he looked down at the glass in his hand and sighed. Kate's eyes were the same shade of brown when she was aroused.

Then again, he scoffed at himself, it might just be her eye color. He couldn't think of a time when they'd been together that her eyes hadn't been that color, or when they'd just spent time together, without fucking.

He grimaced at the thought. Sure, there was nothing

wrong with two adults having sex on the regular. It had been the idea that he'd liked from the beginning. Kate was feisty and she was just as passionate as he was.

Just as hungry too.

That first night replayed in his mind. He'd moved into building C of the apartment building and bumped into Kate in the parking lot after dark. He'd been on his way to the parking lot when she'd literally stumbled into him in the hallway.

After that he hadn't been interested in leaving. A couple of snarky remarks thrown in his direction about his caveman like tendencies and he'd shown her exactly what kind of a caveman he could be.

Remembering the heat of that first time, Rock felt flames dance the length of his neck and up along his jaw.

Kate liked to touch him all over, but when she ate from his mouth, she put her hands on his neck and jaw.

Fuck.

He tossed back the rest of his drink and pushed away from the wall, hoping that the movement would ease some of the strain off of his cock pressed tight against the inside of his zipper.

It did.

A little.

But not enough.

Not even the cold air assaulting his skin could ease off the painful erection his memories had given him.

"Damn it!"

He set the glass on one of the patio tables and reached down to adjust the fit of his jeans. He was so fucked.

Kate's memory kicked in just as she opened the front door of Ciro's. She saw the bunker boot on the bar and the piece of paper taped around the top of the boot.

SETH

She wanted to turn around and walk back home, but it was too late. Pilar would want to know why and really, Kate was just too tired to turn around. She wanted to put her butt in a seat and down a couple of drinks, maybe in that order.

Maybe.

Kate let Pilar get in front of her in line. "Any recommendations?"

Pilar looked at Kate over her shoulder. "You've been here before, right?"

"A while ago." That should be a good enough answer, right?

Pilar gave a non-committal shrug. "Okay..." she looked up at the shelves behind the counter and Kate turned in that direction too. Focus on the matter at hand. Getting a good stiff drink, because getting a good stiff... something or other was going to get her into trouble that she didn't want.

Before they got to the front of the line, Vitalia sidled up to them. "Hey! The cops are here!" She held her hands up. "I'm being good, I promise!"

Pilar shook her head. "Oh well, there goes all the fun. I guess I didn't have to bring my handcuffs after all."

Vitalia set her hand down on Pilar's shoulder. "I love you, woman, but not like that. But... maybe you'd let me borrow those cuffs for... someone else." Kate slid a look toward the back of the room, but she had no idea who Vitalia was singling out because there were about a dozen hot guys in that direction.

Admittedly, Kate didn't give any of them a second look. Sexy? Yeah, they all were. Still, none of them made more of an impact than that.

She really needed to get out more than she did.

"*Anywho*," Vitalia continued, "grab your drinks and come to the back. I'll kick two of the Twenty-Nine guys out of their seats for you."

She leaned in and gave Pilar a kiss on her cheek. "I'll see you guys over there."

She was gone a moment later, enveloped into the shifting crowd.

Pilar shook her head and smiled up at Kate as they stepped forward. "She's like a little star pumping out energy!"

Kate had to admit Pilar was right. "Her parents knew what they were doing when they named her."

Pilar laughed. "Yes! True! So true." Her smile dimmed a little as they moved forward again. "If you want to sit down," her tone was light, but it was hesitant too, "I can bring you your drink."

Kate straightened up and felt her ribs ache in protest. Fucking pride. "No, no. I'm good. I've had worse."

Pilar sighed and shook her head. "You took a good hit. And that guy was big."

Kate's laugh was more of a snort that had them both laughing. "It's going to sting for a day or two, but the Captain is pissed. That's going to hurt for days and days."

"Why is your Captain pissed?"

Oh wow, that voice.

Kate kept her gaze focused ahead of her in the line. "Nothing; it's nothing."

Pilar looked between them and then turned to face the bar as they moved again.

Kate had a moment of hope when Rock kept quiet.

"Kate?"

Please, she begged in silence, leave it alone.

She could feel his heat as he stood behind her. He didn't even need to touch her for every nerve ending to come alive.

She felt his hand touch her hip and she stiffened as need rushed through her. "Not now."

It was an awkward plea, but the instant she felt his hand on her she wanted to lean into him, and she couldn't do that. Not in public. And maybe not in private either. She wanted him too much.

It was becoming a need.

And that, was beyond dangerous.

Bordering on stupid.

He lifted his hand, and she felt the loss of his heat.

They moved forward and reached the bar. Kate was thankful for the distraction.

The man at the bar was her height and she smiled in response to his wide grin. "What can I get for you ladies?"

Kate gestured for Pilar to go first. Her own head was still muddled.

She listened as Pilar ordered a glass of wine and it didn't sound all that appetizing. Kate turned her head towards Rock. "What are you drinking?"

She saw the way that his eyes went from her face to his glass and then turned back to her. "Whiskey." He licked his bottom lip and gave her a half-smile. "Want one?"

She nodded without a word.

She turned back to find the bartender watching them with a thoughtful look.

"Two whiskies, Patrick. And put their drinks on my tab, please."

Too late, Kate realized that Rock had to give his glass

over for his refill. Or maybe her subconscious wanted to torture her. Because when Rock reached for the bar, his chest moved against her back and his arm brushed against hers. He smelled like spice and sin. Heaven help her. She wanted him.

Again.

And that was why she had to move away from him.

Her body didn't move, not even when Rock pressed a glass into her hand. "Thank you."

His smile made her body flood with heat. "Anytime. Glad you decided to come tonight."

Kate found herself walking between Pilar and Rock toward the back of the bar, under all the sea of fairy lights. "Yeah, I... we had a long day."

She gestured at Pilar and thanked her lucky stars that Pilar didn't say much more.

Rock turned his attention to Pilar. "Will Roan be here later?"

A pretty blush made Pilar look flushed. "Yeah. He went home to shower and change, then he's coming."

Rock nodded and Kate could see it out of the corner of her eye. "I'd like to buy him a drink."

A head lifted up from the nearest table. The man was black and gorgeous, almost mouthwatering when his lips curved up into a smile as he stood, showing off a body as good as his face in slacks and a tailored shirt. "Who're you buying a drink for, Rock?" His gaze shifted across all three of them, lighting up at the sight of Pilar. "And who are these ladies?"

"Theo, careful around these two. They're both with the CCPD." Rock gestured toward Pilar. "That's Pilar Bravo. She's engaged, so watch your hands."

Theo, as Rock called him, held up his hands in mock

surrender. "No problem, man." Then he turned his head a little and Kate could see his eyes widen as he looked at her, dipping his gaze to her left hand. "And you? Are you engaged?"

Kate felt a strange tight feeling pull across her cheeks as Rock stiffened at her side.

She had to swallow before she could speak. "Not engaged. Not looking."

Kate caught a spark in Theo's eyes, and he gave her a wink.

"Got it. Keep my hands to myself with both of you beautiful ladies." He looked at Rock again. "Don't worry man, you won't have to rescue either of them from my wicked ways."

Kate felt Rock relax a little.

"I'd happily kick your ass if you tried, but I'd pay to see Kate kick your ass across the street. She's a sergeant in the CCPD."

Theo dipped his chin down and gave her a knowing nod. "I might be okay with that."

Rock moved from her side before Kate could move, but Theo danced back from Rock's reaching hand.

"Behave, Theo."

Theo's laughter lightened the mood. Vitalia may have helped with that too. Appearing beside Theo, she slung her arm across his shoulders.

"Come on, Theo, I can't leave you by yourself for a minute, can I?"

His easy charm flowed like honey. "Sorry, Sis. Can't fault a man for acknowledging beauty where he finds it, can you?"

She sighed loudly. "Lordy, Lordy, Theo. You and I are going to have to talk later." That's when she turned her bright gaze on Kate and Pilar. "You've met Theo Noble, right?"

Vitalia had filled in the final bit of information Kate had been lacking. She extended her hand to Theo, "Not formally, but it works. I'm Kate Turner."

Theo gripped her hand firmly and shook it as he lowered his voice into a sexy purr. "Oh, I work, Kate."

Kate felt Rock suck in a breath beside her. "Wow," she laughed as she freed her hand from his. "Does that work with the ladies?"

Theo put his hand on his chest and winced comically. "She knows how to cut a man deep."

Vitalia brightened and gave Pilar a pointed nod. "Look."

Kate couldn't help but smile as Pilar had to put her hand down on the table and step up on the bottom rung of the chair to boost herself up high enough to see who was in the doorway.

Her officer brightened like a thousand-watt bulb. "Roan!" She waved her hand over her head. "Back here!"

As Kate stepped to the side to make room for Roan between them, she bumped into Rock. He didn't say a word to her. He just set his hand gently on her hip as Roan stepped up to the group.

He gave his fiancé a lingering kiss before addressing the rest of the group. "What did I miss?"

Theo laughed. "Rock warned me off these two ladies. Now I know who put the rock on her finger." He gestured between Pilar and Roan.

Roan nodded. "Glad she decided I was worth it." He turned to Kate. "And what's the secret about you and Ro-"

Kate cleared her throat, but she would enjoy kicking her brother's ass later.

"Roan," she gave him a pointed look before turning back to Theo, "is my brother. Well, one of them."

Theo narrowed his eyes at Roan. "I know you, don't I?"

Someone else stepped up at Theo's side. This man, she knew.

"Chief Campanelli, good to see you."

The man exuded confidence and a generous personality. He was also quite a handsome man with his silvering hair and tanned olive complexion. She'd met him a number of times at events with the CCPD brass. The heads of CCFD and department heads at Cole Medical were always nearby.

And Kate was usually told to attend. Aldo Campanelli always had a kind word and always remembered her name. His wife Gloria too. They were a magnificent couple.

"Sergeant Kate Turner." He took her offered hand and gave it a solid shake. "Good to see you again." He turned to Roan next. "And you, Doctor Ashley. You have our thanks."

Theo rocked back on his heels. "You look different without that Iron Man cap on."

It took Kate a moment to remember what he was talking about. "You still use that surgical cap?"

Roan shrugged. "It does the job, and it was a gift from my sister. Of course, I would."

Theo leaned back and waved at the group behind him. "Hey, guys," he gestured at Roan, "this is the surgeon that operated on Seth, yesterday."

Tables emptied out and hands reached out to shake Roan's hand.

Kate stepped back to make more room, only remembering that Rock was behind her as she was about to set her foot down.

"It's okay," his voice was soft and gentle, "go ahead, I've got you."

She tensed until she felt her foot touch the ground. She sagged back against him before she could think better of it. "Sorry."

"If you're touching me," his voice was a gentle touch against her ear, "you don't ever have to be sorry."

"Hey, you guys want to grab a seat?"

Kate turned toward the voice and saw half a dozen faces smiling at them.

Feeling like she was almost bare naked in front of the group, Kate stepped away and moved toward one of the empty seats that someone had pulled up to the table.

"Thanks." She smiled but she had a feeling that it didn't reach her eyes. "The place is packed tonight." She tried her best to say something sensible. "Is it always like this?"

Theo answered her. "On the weekends, sure. But a weeknight like this? If there's a Cyclones or a Brewers game on, you'll see crowds like this."

"Not a lot of baseball fans in this area?"

A couple of somber looks moved around the table.

She felt more than saw Rock's hand settle on the back of her chair. "After the team's owner moved them out of state, we don't watch the games anymore."

"I guess you can tell I'm not much for sports."

Across the table, a pretty blonde leaned forward. "I am!" When Theo laughed beside her, she gave him a playful elbow. "Hey, don't laugh! I won the betting pool last year in both hockey and football."

The table went eerily silent and Kate understood as soon as Theo turned to look at her with a wincing expression.

"Harmony?"

The blonde turned to look at her friend. "What? It's true! You all lost your money to me when I-"

Vitalia clapped her hand over Harmony's mouth and almost whispered into her ear. "Sweetie, Kate and Pilar are CCPD officers."

Harmony's peaches and cream complexion turned almost green. Regret was easy to read in her eyes.

"Wow," Pilar cleared her throat, "you said that, and I could almost believe you weren't joking."

Kate nodded slowly. "If we had any proof then we'd have to investigate. I doubt we'll ever hear about things like that happening at the firehouse again."

Harmony was statue still on the other side of the table.

Kate felt for the other woman. Working in what is traditionally a man's domain, sometimes you felt like you have to outman the men. "What do you do in the CCFD?"

Harmony managed a smile. "I'm an EMT. We work out of House Twenty-Nine."

Kate nodded. "I bet it's busy in the winter."

Harmony's shoulders relaxed a bit and she nodded, her fingers drawing lines through the condensation on her glass of soda. "Not as many shootings or attacks as the hotter months, but in winter we have more car accidents, heater issues, and worse, a bunch of overdoses. We've never seen so many before."

Overdoses, huh?

Pilar seemed to pick up on it too. "Any particular areas?"

Harmony shrugged. "I'd have to look through our paperwork. I'm usually the passenger. Vega likes to drive."

A few heads nodded in agreement and Kate wondered why she didn't know more people around the table. It wasn't like she had anything against firefighters.

Something Walker said to her popped back up in her head. Her mama bear nature. She really did keep her focus on the officers under her command. Maybe it was time to reach out a little more.

Pilar seemed to have the same idea. "We should talk to someone over in narcotics. See if they'd like to compare the information against what they know."

Kate nodded, her mind already making a note to call Detective Matsumoto. He had a good head on his shoulders. Smart and dedicated to the job.

The jukebox started up and Roan drew Pilar to her feet. Harmony went as well with a guy who walked over nervously wiping his palms on his jeans. Theo didn't move and Kate gave him a curious look.

"Aren't you going to dance?"

Theo's smile was bright, but there was a teasing look in his eyes. "Would you believe I have two left feet?"

She laughed and wagged a finger at him. "You'd be a liar and I know it."

Theo looked at Rock. "She's sharp!"

"And gorgeous."

It felt like Rock's words carried a little heat with them. Heat that she was determined to ignore.

"I would," Theo leaned a little closer to her," but I've been trying to catch someone's eye since I got here, but she keeps looking away."

Kate wasn't usually interested in dating drama. She had enough other drama to bury her under a mountain. Still, as gregarious as Theo was, she couldn't understand why he'd hang back if someone had caught his eyes.

Turning to her side Kate accidentally bumped her ribs against the table. She had to clamp her lips together to try to ignore the pain. She braced her elbow on the table and leaned close to Theo. "Okay, point her out to me."

Theo's laughter was as infectious as it was warm. "What is this? Like a stake out?"

She nodded and gave him a wink before turning back to the room. She had to wonder what was coming over her. She wasn't flirtatious by nature and this wasn't exactly flirting.

Truthfully, it was an easy way to keep from having a more serious conversation with Rock.

Scaredy-cat?

Well, the shoe fit.

"Which one?"

She heard a chair scrape the floor and she could see Theo in her peripheral vision, leaning forward.

"You're the police officer, Kate? You tell me."

Okay, fine. The gauntlet had been thrown.

She sighed and followed up the sound with a slow nod of her head. "Keep in mind that I'm a sergeant in charge of officers on the street, but I've watched enough Sherlock Holmes to have some idea how this is done."

"Oh, yeah," Theo knocked on the tabletop with his knuckles, "bring it."

Letting out a breath, she sat back in her chair and gave a quick look at Rock. The look in his eyes were inscrutable and she turned back to the room as a whole.

"There are a few women here who are obviously with someone, so I'm marking them off the list, because I don't see you going after someone in a relationship."

Theo nodded. "Point to you. That's not my style."

She grinned and continued looking around the room. "There's a small group in the corner. The ones with the satin sashes. They scream bridal shower. That's a no, as well. I doubt they come in here often."

The snort of laughter she heard made her smile.

"You got that right. I bet they're hoping for someone to get drunk enough to strip for them."

She cast a look at the firefighter. "You planning on helping them out?"

He held up his hands in surrender. "No chance. I've got moves, but I save that for a special woman."

"And that special woman..." Kate went back to scanning the crowd and paused on someone seated in the corner of the front façade farthest from the door. When she sat up in her chair to get a better look, the woman stood up, grabbed up her bag, and beat it out the door. "Wow."

She looked back at Theo.

"I have the feeling that I should apologize."

"Not your fault." Theo cleared his throat and slumped back in his seat. "I've seen her here a few times, but when I even think of getting close to her, she's gone."

Before Kate could say anything, Theo set his hands on the tabletop and picked up his empty glass. He gave her a nod. "Kate, nice to meet you. Rock," he slapped a hand on Rock's shoulder, "see you at the House tomorrow. I'm going to go to the hospital and check in on Seth."

Rock gave him a nod and together they watched Theo set the glass on the end of the bar and make his way out the back door to the parking lot.

A quick look around the room told her that Roan and Pilar had stepped off to the side to talk to some of the firefighters in the room. Looking down at her own drink, Kate lifted the glass and took a healthy swallow of the whiskey. It burned but didn't affect her much. Setting it back on the table she looked up and froze.

She hadn't expected Rock to be looking directly at her. "Hey." She smiled but knew it was a feeble attempt. "I didn't mean to chase off your friend."

He gave his head a single shake. "You didn't."

Okay.

Rock shifted in his seat and leaned forward until he braced his forearm on the varnished tabletop. "You want to tell me how you got hurt?"

[3]

ROCK & KATE

"Hurt?" She lifted her glass as if she was going to take another drink but set it down again. "Who said I was hurt?"

He let out a breath, calling on the part of his nature that earned him the name Rock in the first place.

"You leaned against the table. You weren't expecting it to hurt, but it did. I'm guessing that happened because whatever happened was just a few hours ago."

Her startled snort would have been cute if it wasn't for the way her face lost most of its color as she seemed to be fighting to find an answer that she wanted to give.

He wanted to be calm. Goodness knows he'd had plenty of practice growing up, being the one person in the middle of the maelstrom who didn't buckle.

It was harder than normal this time. He could walk through a building on fire and not flinch. His heart rate hardly went above normal even in the direst of circumstances, but one wince from Kate and his heart was pounding in his chest.

"It's just a part of the job." Her words were meant to

reassure, or put him off the question, but they failed on both counts.

"I could go over there and cut in on Roan."

She tensed as he continued.

"I bet Pilar would tell me."

Kate's eyes narrowed and her words clipped out between her teeth. "I hope not."

He reached out a hand to touch her but set it on the table between them when she started to pull back. "Then tell me, Kate. I won't bite."

There was no mistaking the sudden flare of heat in her eyes. He had to work to keep focus on the matter at hand. Sex wasn't a possibility. Not until he knew what was wrong.

She shook her head. "You might hear about it anyway." The disappointment in her voice was palpable. "I was called to a domestic dispute to back up two of my officers. It had been simple at first. A father was late returning his daughter to her mother. Jo and Matt were the ones called to the scene and spoke to the father. They got him to bring the little girl out of the house, but before they could get her turned over to her mom, the stepdad showed up.

"Matt and Jo stepped in and got the stepdad to hang back, but seeing him, the ex went crazy. He probably would have taken all three of them down."

"And you stepped in."

She shrugged in that way she always did to brush things off. "He's a big guy. And if I hadn't... done what I did, it might have ended up worse."

"But you got hurt instead."

She shook her head, but he could tell she was just going through the motions.

"Did you go to the ER?"

She hesitated, but before he could say anything, she

continued. "I had to go. It wasn't because I thought I was really hurt," she stumbled a bit as her words rushed on, "but I needed the report from the hospital for the brutality complaint."

He could tell by the way her face blanched that she hadn't meant to say what she had.

"Look," she got up from her chair and tossed back the rest of her drink, "forget I said anything. Okay? I could blame it on the drink if I'd had more than a couple fingers, but the point is I can't... I just can't."

With that she turned away and set the glass on the edge of the bar and reached into her pocket for the twenty she always kept there. When she passed by Patrick at the front, she gave him the bill. "For Seth."

He nodded and thanked her, but he cast a curious glance over her shoulder. That got her moving faster.

The last thing she wanted to do was run from Rock. Not because it was him. She didn't run from anything. Ever.

She didn't want anyone to see what was going on between them.

Her steps stuttered as she came to the street and she swore under her breath.

Luck held out and there was a gap in traffic on the street giving her a chance to move across before anything happened.

Because that's what was happening between her and Rock. "Nothing."

Kate reached the opposite curb before she looked back and that's when she saw him standing on the sidewalk on her side of the street. He didn't know how much it hurt to see him there. She wanted him to be that man. The kind that worried about her.

Cared.

But it was the other side of the coin that she feared. Dreaded, really. When he wouldn't care.

When he was tired of her.

And done.

That was something she couldn't... wouldn't go through.

She lived her entire adult life that way and it had worked. Until Rock.

He was the one that wanted to cross the line.

Lifting her chin, she gave him what she hoped was a look that told him not to come any closer.

A look that said she was putting that wall firmly between them.

Sure, if he could keep to their agreement, she wasn't ruling anything out. She liked what they had. Craved it... from time to time.

Shaking herself free of her morbidly needy thoughts she turned and continued to walk down the street heading home.

A bath would be perfect. Hot water. Epsom salts. She could soak until the pain went away or until she didn't care anymore and climbed into bed to sleep it off.

It felt like it took forever to walk the one block over and get into her floor-level apartment.

In the privacy of her room, she reached down, unhooked the button at the waist of her jeans and let out a sigh. The zipper came down with a soft whisper of relief and that's when it hit her.

Desire.

There hadn't been any warning. Just a soft sound she'd

heard thousands of times before, but the reaction was nothing she was used to.

She wanted him. Wanted to be touched by him. Wanted him to soothe her aches and pains. If she'd let him in...

She pushed at her jeans and got them over her hips and almost to her thighs when the pain lanced through her side.

"Fuck." She repeated the word a handful of times as she tried to find the right position of her body so that it wouldn't give her pain.

And even when she managed to find a better position, it still hurt. She wasn't going to take a bath. She had already taken a shower in the locker room at the Precinct before the bruising really started to form.

Kate managed the buttons down the front of her blouse easily enough. Shrugging it off of her shoulders wasn't all that bad, but the instant that she tried to lift the bottom hem of her camisole she knew she'd been beat.

There was no way that she was going to pull it off on her own.

She grumbled at herself and left it on. She wasn't even going to try to change into a nightshirt. All she wanted to do was flop down onto the bed and sleep. Out cold would be good, but her mind was too loud to sleep just yet.

Moving over to the bed, she didn't even bother to pull the blanket down. She set a knee down and braced her hands on the center of the bed, managing a few shuffling movements before she fell, face down with a wince.

Kate groaned and made a sound that sadly sounded like a whimper. "Owww."

Big bad police sergeant?

Not so much.

She was used to sucking it up throughout her life. Once

she went to the police academy she had to 'man up' or be thought of as less than the men. Pain? She could take it.

But she could also let it go when she was alone.

Letting out a breath, she closed her eyes and tried to let it all go.

Breath in.

Breath out.

The pain sat there along her ribs like a brick.

For a moment, she considered getting up and grabbing a few pain pills from the medicine cabinet, but the instant that she tried to move she knew that wasn't going to happen.

She was stuck.

And frustrated.

Thank goodness her phone was somewhere on the floor or she might have been tempted to call Rock and ask him to come back.

She really was having a hard time closing the door between them.

The clock on the wall ticked away and while the room was dark, she was still wide awake, humming.

Her blood rushing through her veins as she wiggled a little on the bed, placing her head on the opposite pillow.

A deep breath in was all she needed to remember that Rock had fallen asleep there, spooned up behind her.

Now, she was aching in a different way.

The scent of him on her pillow made her feel hot all over.

Hot.

Hungry.

And so damn alone.

Slipping her hand under the hem of her camisole, she brushed her palm over her belly, remembering the feel of his hand against her skin.

Remembered the words he'd whispered in her ear as he'd rubbed up against her back and the feel of his body, hard against hers.

There was something so perfect about a man who was hard in all the right places.

Her hand slipped down, fingers working between her legs. The elastic pull of her waistband kept her wrist and arm tight to her body and made it easier to reach-

Yes.

Right there.

The feel of her fingers had been enough before, it would have to be again.

Faster. Deeper.

She squeezed her eyes shut and pulled her lower lip between her teeth as her fingers found a rhythm that had her riding the edge.

But Kate just couldn't get over that edge.

She rolled, sandwiching her arm between her and the bed, pushing her fingers deeper, but no matter how much she tried she couldn't get there.

A groan pulled from her lips and a curse followed it.

Still, nothing.

Kate pulled in a ragged breath and her senses were flooded with the scent of Rock's skin, the clean scent of his cologne.

Her nipples were diamond hard, pressing against the soft fabric of her camisole and her fingers plunged deep into her body. She came, tensing and then shuddering with the rush of sensations that burned through every inch of her body.

A soft sob burst from her lips and she buried her face in his pillow.

It was enough to make her cry, but she was too exhausted. Bone deep exhausted.

And heaven help her, she wanted him.

She wanted to call him back.

Kate fell asleep reeling from the fact that Rock wasn't the only one who had stepped across the line, violated their agreement.

She was just as guilty as he was.

And it had to stop.

○+※✱♝

Rock knocked softly on the frame of the door. "Is everything okay?"

Shifting in his chair by the hospital bed, Lieutenant Isaac MacKenzie fought off a yawn and stood up.

Rock tried to wave him back down. "You don't have to get up."

Isaac shook his head and stretched. Rock heard an audible pop from his back. "It's good. I needed to stand up before my legs fell completely asleep." He couldn't fight off a yawn the second time. "Damn, what time is it?"

Rock didn't even look at his watch. "Late or early, whichever way you want to look at it."

Isaac nodded, but Rock could tell his mind was already drifting away.

"You want to take a walk or go home for a few hours, man?" Rock gestured at the chair. "I can stay for a while."

Isaac started to shake his head and then he hesitated. "I can stay."

Rock set his hand on Isaac's shoulder. "Come on, Faust. You need to get some sleep. If you fall out of the chair and crack your head open, you're not going to be able to function. We need you."

His head tipped forward and his shoulders hunched over. Rock swore he could feel the weight pressing down on Isaac.

"I don't... I don't know if I'm the right man for this job."

Rock heard the anguish in his friend's words, and he understood it. Seth was Isaac's oldest friend. They'd grown up together; just a few houses separated their homes while they'd been growing up. They were both extremely good at what they did. Together they could scale buildings and walls. Seth was a little thinner than Isaac, more lanky than muscular and when there were small places that they needed to fit for a rescue, Seth never waited for anyone to tell him what to do. He waded in. The victims, the people at risk, were always his focus.

"You know that's crap. Seth would tell you to shut up and man up." Rock felt for Isaac, he'd been nearly frantic when the wreck shifted and pinned Seth in the car. "Remember, you were the one who literally pulled him out of that heap *after* you found a way for us to stabilize it. He's never been one to hold back, not when there was someone in trouble."

"Maybe I should have held him back. He didn't wait for me to evaluate the situation."

It hurt Rock to the core that Isaac was torturing himself over this.

"You were already busy trying to get that kid out of his car seat. He knew he should have waited." Rock blew out a breath through his nose, frustrated at his own inability to ease the strain for his lieutenant. "I know that's cold comfort, but Seth did what he did because that's what he's always done. What both of you always do. You dive in and fix it."

"That got us this far," Isaac sighed, "but what if 'what works' ends his career? What if he can't walk after this?"

Rock folded his arms across his chest, struggling to keep his calm. "Is that what the doctors are saying? He's paralyzed?"

"No." Isaac shook his head. "No. Not yet. The surgery was good. It fixed the worst of the problems, but there's swelling that no one counted on. They have him on medication, but his pain levels are killing him." Isaac looked back at the bed for a moment and then turned away. The lines in his forehead looked deeper. "They had to knock him out and pump him full of meds to help speed the healing."

"So, there's hope. Focus on that."

A soft shifting sound reached their ears from a dark corner of the room.

Isaac turned and his gaze slid in that direction.

Rock turned and followed his gaze. He couldn't help but smile at what he saw.

Vitalia Campanelli was curled up and asleep across two chairs that had been pulled together with the chair backs at her head and feet. Rock could see Isaac's leather jacket covering her like a blanket for the most part, but there was no mistaking her wild curls against the pale chair.

When Isaac spoke, his voice had softened from his gruff self-incrimination. "She came over to tell me how things went at Ciro's."

"Yeah?" He nodded. "I was there earlier. There was a good turn out."

"Yeah. She told me she arranged for cover on her next shift to stay here in case Seth needs anything."

"She's family." Rock had known Vitalia for half of her

life. His earliest memories were of her hanging out at the station house after basketball practice or dance class, her hair in ever-present braids and a big ear-to-ear smile.

"She's always there for us." Isaac shook his head. "As if she doesn't have enough going on in her life."

"She cares about you more than any of us. You know that."

Isaac's laugh almost sounded like a cough. He shook his head and turned away, his eyes straying to her sleeping form again. "It's because of her dad."

Rock leaned back and narrowed his eyes. "The Chief? What does he-"

"Those dinners? Sunday nights at his house. Chief always keeps us close. Of course, Lia would get close to us. We're like a whole house of brothers to her."

"Family? Sure." Rock was trying to hedge his answer, taking care not to smack his lieutenant across the face with the truth, not right at that moment. It wouldn't do any good. He already had his walls up, struggling with Seth's injuries. Still, he couldn't completely ignore the truth that most of the house knew. "You really think of her as a sister?"

"Don't we all?" Isaac turned around and took a few steps back toward the bed before stopping. "Could you take her home? I bet the Chief would like to make sure she gets home safe."

"Have you been home at all?" Rock didn't even wait for an answer, he knew what it was. "Take her home, you know the Chief will tell you to stay in the guest room. Get some sleep."

Rock could see Isaac wavering. He wanted to say no. He wanted to stay for his friend.

"I'll stay here." Rock made the offer easily. Kate wanted

her space and he'd give it to her, no matter how much he hated to do it. "If anything big happens, I'll call."

Rock thought he could see some relief in Isaac's expression and then a solid set to the Lieutenant's shoulders as he made the decision.

"Yeah, I'll take her home." He looked up at Rock and held out his hand. "Thanks, man."

Rock shook his hand and gave him a solid clap on his shoulder. "Good. I'll make sure there's someone here at all times. Go. You both need some real rest."

He stood off to the side as Isaac tried to figure out how to lift Vitalia from the chair without waking her up. Isaac's concern said more than anything about his connection to the Chief's only biological child.

Sure, Chief Campanelli meant it when he said they were all family to him, but Vitalia was the light of his life.

Rock remembered when the chief found out that she'd applied and was accepted to the Academy. He'd shut himself in his office after reading the bulletin pinned to the board in the community room.

He would walk into hell with each and every man and woman under his command, but that was the last thing he'd ever wanted for his daughter.

"Huh? What?"

Vitalia was a little confused as Isaac helped her stand up. He had to soothe her worries first. Waking up in the half dark of the room, she needed to hear about Seth before she allowed Isaac to steer her toward the door. Her sleepy half-wave toward Rock made him smile and return the gesture.

Watching the two walk out of the room, Rock shook his head and sighed. He understood the way Vitalia cuddled in against Isaac's side, saw the truth of her feelings in her wide eyes as she gazed up at Isaac. His lieutenant might care for her, but Vitalia was in love with Isaac.

It was a recipe for disaster unless something happened to get his friend to see her as a woman and not just his 'sister'.

Lord knows he suffered from the same ailment as Vitalia. He was in love with someone who didn't return his affections.

"Life sucks, huh?"

Rock turned to the bed and smiled. "Hey, man. You're awake."

Before Seth lifted his hand to gesture him forward, Rock was already walking. When he reached the railing, he reached out a hand.

"I was awake a while ago." Seth grabbed it with his and Rock felt a flicker of strength in his friend's grip. "I was hoping Faust would fall asleep or someone would kick him out and take his mood with him."

Rock grabbed a hold of the chair that Isaac had been sitting in and pulled it closer to the bed. "What happened?"

Seth waved his hand vaguely in the air. "He's blaming himself."

Rock sat back in his chair and stretched his legs out before him. "I'd like to say that's crazy-"

"But that's Faust." They ended the sentence together and Seth gave him a rueful smile.

"Did he say it was anything specific that he thought he could have done?"

Seth seemed to sag into the bed, exhausted. "He doesn't have a reason. Fuck if he needs one to feel responsible."

Rock felt for his friends. There was a deep and abiding friendship between Seth and Isaac. One born of their shared childhood and solidified in the last few years as they worked together saving lives, having each other's back. They'd all faced danger together and there had been times when death had shared the same space with them, eagerly waiting over their shoulders for its chance to exact the last and most permanent toll.

Oblivion.

"You want me to talk to him?" Rock braced himself for the inevitable answer.

Seth closed his eyes and shook his head. "You could talk yourself blue in the face and he'll still shoulder that yoke and strap it to his back with chains. I need you to do me a favor though."

"Anything, man. You know it." Rock's hands lifted from his thighs and he sat forward, dropping them onto his knees. The soft and well-worn denim of his jeans helped to settle himself, determined to help in any way he could.

Seth's eyes blinked and Rock could swear he saw tears in his eyes, but he didn't draw attention to it. He could tell that Seth was tiring and the last thing he wanted to do was put more strain on him.

"Can you just keep an eye on him?" Seth stifled a yawn. "I know we joke about him being the luckiest man alive, but I worry that he's going to push himself to the point where that luck is going to run out. I need someone to have eyes on him, okay?"

Rock nodded, a solemn drop of his chin. "You know I'll be there, man. We always have each other's backs. The two of you tend to jump in sometimes and forget that we're all there for you. Niko, Halo, Reese... we'll be there for him. You keep yourself on the mend. Relax and heal. We'll be there waiting when you're ready to come back."

It was impossible to miss the dark look that passed over his features and it took a moment too long for him to speak.

"We'll see what the doctors say, but I'll handle that, Rock. I need you to be there for him and haul his ass out of the fire if you have to."

Rock bobbed his head in an easy acknowledgment of his words. "It goes without saying. Close your eyes. Get some rest. I can sit out in the hall if it will make you feel better."

Seth held his hand out and Rock didn't like the way it shook before he clasped it in his own. "Go ahead and stay if you like. I'm going to knock out. At least you won't stare at me like I'm about to die on you."

He let go of Seth's hand and pointed at the door. "I'm gonna step out for a minute and grab a cup of coffee. Go to sleep."

He had a feeling that Seth was asleep before he set foot in the hallway and he was glad. He could see how much pain he was in and Seth was fighting to hide it as best as he could.

Rock was halfway down the hall before he realized that he was heading in the wrong direction. He started to turn around at the nursing station when he heard a familiar voice.

"Rock? What are you doing here?" She stepped up to the counter with a frown. "Is something wrong with Seth?"

He smiled at her question. Xiomara Ortiz was the head of orthopedic surgery at Cole Medical and she'd been the lead on Seth's most recent surgery. She had a heart of gold like the majority of the staff at the hospital. "He's a little shaky," he confided in her, "and I'm worried about him. He doesn't seem to think he's going to come back from this."

Rock's stomach twisted at her silence.

It turned into a distinct ache as she tried to school her expression. "You know I can't give you details." She held up her hand to ward off his denial. "I know... you're all family, but I can't break the rules like that. If Seth didn't tell you, I can't disclose it. I just want you to know that we are doing everything... *everything* we can for him. He's going to need your support," she gave him a strong look that didn't make room for any argument, "just like your house always does. We're still early in this and when the swelling goes down, we'll be able to really see what's going on. That's as much as I can tell you."

He couldn't argue with that.

"Okay. I get it. And if there's anything we can do for him. Just let us know."

"Patience," she explained, "and your presence, will do wonders for him."

Rock lifted a hand and rubbed at the back of his neck where the tension had sunk in and pinched at his nerves. "Thanks again, Doctor."

Her expression softened. "No need to be so formal, Rock. You can call me Xiomara, or Mara if it's easier."

"Mara?" He shook his head. "Xiomara may be a little bit of work, but it fits you better." Maybe it was the bright fluorescent lights weighing down on them, but he thought he saw a little color in her cheeks. "Thanks again."

She shrugged. "Just doing my job. You can come and talk to me anytime. And I promise you I'll check in with Seth and make sure that we're keeping his pain at a manageable level."

Before he could say anything else, he heard a soft tone and she reached into her coat for her phone. A quick look was all she needed.

"Sorry, I've got to go. I'll see you later."

"Yeah. Later." He watched her go and blew out a breath. Something was going on with Seth, something he didn't want to talk about. Rock didn't want to push his friend, but he worried that Seth would try to deal with everything on his own and that wasn't going to happen.

Rock was going to watch Isaac's back, but he was also going to do the same for Seth. When they called House Twenty-Nine a family, they meant it, and Rock was determined to prove it.

[4]

ROCK & KATE

Rock's next shift was a pain and a half. Everyone was still on edge and worried about Seth when they were at the Station House, but once they were on the second half of the twenty-four-hour shift things had evened out.

Most of it anyway.

Everyone except for their floater Desmond Lofton. He was having the time of his life. He hadn't even slept overnight, something that a few of them were trying not to think about. However, the fact was driven home when Rock drew the short straw and had to make breakfast for the shift.

He had to go through the lounge to get to the kitchen from the bunkrooms and as soon as he opened the door, he saw the floater with his feet up on one of the tables and a game controller in his hands.

"This is the shit!" He turned his gaze back to the TV on the wall. "Wow, this house is awesome!"

Rock rolled his eyes. "Just keep your voice down. The Lieutenant is just a little way down the hall. If you wake him up after the last few days we've had, he's going to throw you through that TV screen. Is this a thing you have?"

Desmond shrugged. "Not sleeping?"

Rock flexed a muscle in his jaw and blew out a breath. "Being a hyper mess."

"Hyper Mess," he mused. "Too long for a good nickname."

Rock shook his head. "You want a nickname? How about you focus on the job and not 'the experience.' Okay?"

He walked through the archway toward the kitchen, stopping just shy of the kitchen door. "Hey, Lofton?"

"What?"

"Since you're up, come on. Give me a hand."

The floater grumbled but he got up and marched himself into the kitchen. Thank god he didn't need more instruction than pointing him at the refrigerator and the words 'scrambled eggs.' That let Rock focus his head on the matter bothering him the most.

He hadn't needed his alarm to wake him up for kitchen duty. He'd already been up for an hour or so. Rock hadn't been able to sleep all that well. He had questions in his mind about Kate and what had happened to her on duty.

Rock had reviewed the footage on his phone while Seth slept.

Someone passing through the area had taken a video of the incident and broadcast it on social media.

At that point, the comments were split on who was at fault and who should be blamed for the clash. Both father and stepfather had their share of supporters and detractors.

As for Kate, most of the comments were positive in her favor. He knew it wasn't going to stay that way. So, when he got up early, he'd gone back online looking for information.

The video was on more sites and the number of comments had gone through the roof. It was obvious to him in the footage that Kate got in the middle to stop a fight from happening. Those early comments had reflected that.

But somewhere from the time he'd gone back to his place to get ready for shift and just an hour ago, things had devolved.

One of the commentators had a few choice words about her.

> *BBoy69: bitch better not put her hands on me like that*
> *JOES321: I dunno, man. I like a woman who gets handsy*
> *BBoy69: I'll tell you what she can do with her hands and then I'll show her what I can do with my-*

"Rock? You think I should put some cut up veggies in the scrambled eggs?"

He turned to look at the other man. "Just scramble the eggs."

Desmond seemed a little deflated at the answer. "Yeah, okay. Sorry."

Rock shook his head. "Look. If you like it here and want to stick around for a few shifts, you're going to have to try to blend in. We're all a little upset and worried about Seth. Making things crazy isn't helping."

Desmond mustered a smile. "Yeah, okay. Got it! You rock, Rock."

Rock shut him out with a shake of his head.

It had actually been a good thing that his mind had been pulled out of his thoughts. The conversation, if you could call it that, continued on for quite a bit with more men getting involved. Men who didn't think a woman had business being a law enforcement officer. Men who thought she should stick to the jobs a woman belonged in. Housewife. Hooker. Those types of guys.

Those guys who wouldn't know what to do with a real woman if they had the chance.

They were assholes and there were a lot of them.

Rock reached over and turned on the fan above the flattop to siphon the smoke away from the griddle and yes, the fire alarm.

He used the spatula to push the first line of bacon out of the hotspot and onto the top edge while he started another line of bacon, peeling each one off of the stack that they came in from the big box store.

Rock was sure that Kate had seen the coverage and the comments. Her boss had probably shoved them in her face as he liked to do when similar things popped up.

It wasn't an unfair judgment for Rock to make.

Kate hadn't told him anything about the way her Captain treated her, but he knew the man. The Captain was long on self-interest and short on loyalty to the people who worked under him.

He'd heard better things about Commissioner Zerbe. He was fair, balanced, and a defender of the CCPD. The problem was, to get to the Commissioner, Kate would have to go through her Captain and Catalano didn't let much go up above his head.

Reading the horrible, vile things that people said about Kate, not just calling into question what she'd done, but also the nasty things they said about her as a person pissed him off.

Rock ground his teeth together. Those people making those comments didn't see her as a person. They saw her as a target. Something less than a human.

He slid a glance toward the counter where he'd left his phone. Part of him wanted to send a text to Pilar and ask her to keep an eye on Kate for him, but he knew that it wouldn't likely stay between the two of them.

Pilar would likely tell Roan. Those two didn't keep secrets between them.

It was something he was jealous about.

When Pilar and Roan were first working things out between them, he and Kate had been spending a lot of time together.

And he could tell that they were different from the other couple in so many ways.

When Pilar and Roan were together, they didn't feel the need to say what they weren't to each other. Not the way Kate did to him.

About him.

About *them*.

He still didn't understand exactly why she didn't want a relationship. All he could do was hope that it wasn't about him, exactly. That whatever it was holding her back wouldn't always be a line that she'd draw between them.

But after reading the comments about her... and to her... online, he wondered if that was a possibility.

What people said about her was dehumanizing and there was no way to avoid thinking about it.

The man that she'd confronted the first time that Rock met her had spouted epithets like that. He'd called Kate all kinds of names and Kate had brushed it off. Laughing sometimes as the man hurled insults and spat at her feet.

He didn't know how she managed to hold it all in. How do you face that kind of hate and rage and keep cool and calm? Kate had to have a backbone of steel to deal with that every day on the street.

"Oh, hey... Look at the TV. Isn't that the thing that happened the other day?"

Letting out a huff of air, Rock grudgingly lifted his gaze to the TV and felt his heart constrict in his chest. "Can you turn up the volume?"

"I didn't think it was that important." With a shrug, Desmond picked up the remote and clicked the volume button a few times.

On screen, the newscaster was in the middle of their opening spiel.

"...with public opinion becoming critical of CCPD's Sergeant Kate Turner, we were able to gain permission to speak to the woman at the center of the fight that day."

Rock couldn't even remember what the woman had looked like in the video. Actually, he hadn't really paid much attention to her. His focus had been on Kate the whole time.

Talk about blinders.

Seated on a bench in a park, the woman looked like she was just a few moments from losing whatever food she had in her stomach. The name was printed in bold letters: MICHELLE N. They'd avoided using her full last name on the chyron and he didn't blame her. There would be enough people who would know who she was by sight. He understood wanting to keep those people to a minimum.

The reporter was off screen and had the large, foam-covered microphone held out in front of Michelle's face. "From what I understand, Michelle. You're telling us that your ex-husband is... being deceptive, that the officer didn't use unnecessary force in subduing him?"

Michelle started to shake her head and stopped. She started to nod and stopped, likely realizing that either gesture would be confusing. When she opened her mouth to speak her voice was soft, but it was also clear. "That video doesn't show everything that was happening. If it did," she swallowed visibly, "then there wouldn't be a question. That policewoman did everything she could to keep the situation from turning into a fight." Michelle sucked in a breath and a sob punctuated the end of it. "I didn't want my baby to see her father mad. I didn't want her to see any more bloodshed. He's never been very kind, but he's managed to keep that side of himself from our little girl."

The microphone disappeared out of frame and the reporter was heard again. "So, in your opinion, the actions of Sergeant Turner were appropriate?"

The young mother on the screen nodded, her eyes misting with tears. "If it hadn't been for her... if she hadn't gotten in the middle and stopped him in his tracks..." her voice hitched, and she covered her face with her hands. "Oh my god! My baby."

Rock felt his throat tighten as a little girl appeared at the edge of the frame. Her face was the perfect study in confusion and caring. Leaning into her mother's side, the little girl wrapped her arms around her mother's middle and gave her a big squeeze.

"It's okay, Mommy! We're okay."

Michelle dropped her arm gently around her daughter's shoulders and pulled the little girl into her side. "I know, baby. I know. Sorry. Mommy was scared, but we're okay now."

The camera remained on the two as they comforted each other, and the reporter's voice came through as a voice over to the tender scene. "This is Kennedy Heart with WCCN News on Channel Twelve. Reporting about Center City from the Heart."

Kate leaned her head against the tiled wall of the restroom and let out a breath.

The interview that was making its rounds on social media had gone a long way to letting her off the hook for the negative publicity generated by the intervention she'd made the other day.

It wasn't going to die down anytime soon though.

That was the nature of these things.

Your average person on the street would see the interview and accept the information and let it ease their worry about what she'd been accused of. Unfortunately, there was a whole other group of people that would turn a deaf ear to what Michelle said.

A soft knock on the door reached her ears.

"Come in." Kate sighed and started to pull herself together. She still had a few hours to go in her shift.

Tossing the paper towel into the trash can, she lifted her chin and fixed a smile on her face. It was easy to put on a brave face. She had that gesture down pat.

Pilar stepped in and closed the door. "Hey, Roan's outside. He wants to know if you have time for lunch with us."

Kate looked down at her uniform. "I don't know. Being on desk duty, I think I should stay here at the precinct. You two go and have a nice lunch."

She wasn't begging off for her. The last thing Kate wanted was for Pilar to experience the same treatment she had on the street earlier. Just showing up at work had been a circus. A couple of yahoos followed her down the street from her parking spot, calling out a slew of words that made it very clear what they thought of her actions. She would be lucky to find her car undamaged when she left the station at the end of her shift.

Pilar's smile didn't falter a bit. "We had a feeling you'd say that, so he brought in some food from Peggy Ann's. Conference room is open." She tilted her head toward the door. "Let's go."

It was a damn sight better than eating alone.

The smile Kate put on her face was the first real one of the day. "That man of yours isn't half bad."

Pilar flushed a warm pink under her tan skin. "I might just keep him."

Kate shared a laugh with Pilar as they walked out of the bathroom, and neither of them spared a look for the curious stares turned in their direction.

Her heart lightened at the easy exchange and when they neared the conference room, she saw her brother Roan. He stood up, smiling and approached the door, pulling it open for them. Leaning forward, he shared a gentle kiss with Pilar after making sure the way was clear.

Then, as Kate stepped up, he gave her a hug. He held on for a moment longer than normal and leaned in to ask her. "You okay?"

"Careful," she moved out of his arms and gave his arm a swat as she closed the door, "people are going to think I'm not the big bad Sergeant if they think I need hugs from my little brother."

Predictably, Roan made a show of looking down at her from his height. "Little?"

She poked him in the arm. "Keep that up and I'll take you down to the ground."

Roan surprised her with his laugh as he gestured at a chair. "I don't know, Kate. I've had a tutor. And I might have a few tricks to get the upper hand."

Kate slid into the chair and gave Pilar a mock-stern look. "Not fair."

Pilar shrugged and handed her a to-go cup of coffee. "He didn't tell me he was going to use the skills on you."

Kate gave them both a baleful look. "Likely story."

They dug into their food and kept the conversation light. It was the best time she'd had all day, until her brother said something out of left field.

"So, I heard from mom today."

Kate heard Pilar's stiff intake of breath but didn't acknowledge it. Instead, offering up a question of her own. "What's the news from home?"

Roan turned his gaze toward Pilar and Kate felt bad for both of them. She knew that they were both worried about that first meeting with the Turners. Roan had already met the Bravos and Pilar's elder brother who was in the FBI. Of course, it had been when she was in the hospital recovering from a gunshot wound. That had been fraught enough for him, but Kate knew that Pilar was really anxious about meeting Roan's mother and Kate's father.

Leaning against the table, Roan reached out his hand and covered Pilar's. "Mom decided that she's not going to wait for us to find time in our schedules to go and see them. They're coming to see us here in Center City."

Kate didn't miss the nervous tug of Pilar's hand under Roan's. She shook her head and leaned in. "Hey, you need to relax," she told the younger officer. "They're going to love you, okay? Seriously. My dad? He's all about what makes Cora happy. And Cora? She's going love you because you make her favorite son happy."

"Seriously? Her favorite?"

Kate looked up at Walker standing in the doorway. "I said what I said, little bro."

Walking in like he owned the place, Walker Ashley reached into the bag on the table and took out a handful of fries. He backed away until his butt hit the chair rail on the wall. "You just said that because I was standing there." He pushed a couple of fries into his mouth. "These are cold."

Roan looked up at their brother. "Because they weren't for you. I came to see Pilar and Kate."

Walker's mouth dropped open and Kate covered her eyes.

"Close your mouth!"

She didn't hear a word, but she suddenly smelled vegetable oil, salt, and Walker's soap. His laughter followed.

"But I'm your favorite, right? Sarge?"

She shot her hand out and connected with something hard.

"Ow!"

Kate opened her eyes and saw Walker pressing his hands up against his belly, wincing at her. "Sorry. Not sorry. Keep your fry breath to yourself."

He straightened up pretty quickly and snagged another handful of fries. "What did I miss before I came in? There were some sullen faces in the room." He turned to look at Kate. "Did Catalano chew you out again? I thought that interview was pretty good."

Kate blew out a breath. She really didn't want to be reminded about it.

Roan took over, steering the conversation away from her. "I heard from Mom. They're coming to Center City in a little over a week-"

"A week?" Pilar looked a little pale. "That's soon." She turned her gaze toward Kate. "That's really soon."

Kate gave Roan a pointed look. "That would have been nice to know from the start, hmm?"

He shrugged. "It's not a big deal. They already love you," he directed the gentle comment to Pilar, "because I love you."

Walker made a sound in his throat like he was choking but managed to lean away and avoid another shot to his stomach from Kate. She glared at him. "Stuff it, scruffy."

Lifting a hand to his chin, Walker made a point to scratch at his chin. "Hey, I trim."

He did manage to keep his goatee trimmed and it gave him a kind of devilish air about him, but she rarely passed up the opportunity to rile him up when she could.

"Whatever." She rolled her eyes. "Be supportive or get the hell out."

Before Walker could make a snarky comment, Roan looked over at his brother. "It's good you stopped by. Mom had a message for you too."

Kate couldn't help but laugh at him. "Uh oh."

Walker narrowed his eyes at her in a heated glare.

Roan continued to speak in the middle of their childish battle.

"They're planning a small family dinner."

Kate latched onto the idea and gave Pilar a gentle pat on her arm. "See? Six people. You'll have us there to-"

"Eight."

"I'm sorry, what?" It took Kate a minute to understand what he was saying. "Eight?"

"Eight." Roan gave her a hopeful smile. "They want you and Walker to bring a date."

"No!"

Kate felt her heart stutter in her chest. She didn't even have to look at Walker to know his reaction. After all, they'd both declared a rather emphatic no just a moment ago.

Walker grumbled in his customary way. "No. I'm not

bringing a woman to dinner with our parents. You?" He looked at Kate and she shook her head.

"I'm not bringing anyone either. You know what would happen." She turned to Roan. "You know your mom would be prying into things. And whatever schmuck I'd even be tempted to ask would just run for the hills. No amount of promised booze would make a guy suffer a dinner with parents!"

Kate saw Pilar start to open her mouth to speak and Kate got to her feet.

"Look, thanks for lunch. It was great to see you, Roan. Don't bring this up again. Bye now."

Yes, she walked out with her back ramrod straight and her steps a little too fast to even hope she looked strong and confident, but the boys were family and Pilar soon would be too, legally, since Kate already cared for the other woman like family.

They already knew she was upset, and they knew the reason why. And even if they'd never discussed it in front of others, they knew what she was running from. Her Achilles heel, her lack of a relationship.

Cora had tried to broach the subject before. She had a way of making everything easier to hear, but that didn't mean that Kate wanted to talk about it, ever.

Kate didn't stop until she'd made her way back to the desk downstairs in reception. Being on desk duty would normally give her hives, but since it was the one thing that stood between her and her family's *helpful* suggestions, she wanted to hug the old, scarred-wooden surface and the eternally empty cup of pencils that teetered back and forth with every shift of weight on the desktop.

The front doors of the precinct opened up and two of her officers came in out of the cold. Officer Josephine Swan was followed by her partner for the day, Burke Pelton. The two stopped at the edge of her desk and Josephine spoke first. "It's damn cold outside, Sergeant."

Burke scoffed and folded his arms across his chest. "Told you to get thermals for under the uniform."

She turned on her partner and gave him a wide-eyed stare. "I went to the uniform store, but they're out of small sizes. They say they're waiting on a shipment, and," she gave a little extra emphasis to the word, probably to stop Burke from interjecting his own answer, "I've already shopped at regular stores and the prices are killer."

Burke bit his lips and Kate had to give him silent props for keeping whatever was in his head to himself. After Pilar's shooting, he'd turned his attitude around. At least in public and in front of other officers. Kate could only hope that he'd continue to be on his best behavior when he was in uniform.

Still, she knew she had to divert the conversation. He didn't need any temptation. "What happened on your patrol?"

Josephine took point and walked Kate through the interactions they had and the two arrests that they'd made on patrol.

Burke interjected a few pertinent details and by the time they were finished she gave them both a satisfied nod. "Go ahead and type up your reports. Leave them on my desk before you go, and I'll review them before shift starts tomorrow."

Burke let out a long breath, but she wouldn't have known if she hadn't been watching him surreptitiously. "Thanks, Sergeant. We'll have them to you before we leave."

Josephine nudged him with her shoulder. "Lookit you! All polite and stuff. I like it, Burke!"

He snarled a little at the praise.

Josephine gave Kate a big grin. "I hope you're off desk duty tomorrow, Sarge. It shouldn't take them much longer to realize you were a hero."

Kate sighed. "I don't want to be a hero, Joe. I just don't want to be the villain."

Nodding, Josephine smiled at her, but the smile didn't have her usual luster. "I hear you, Sarge. Still, we know you were a hero. That little girl didn't need to see her two dads fighting. You did what you could."

Kate felt an unfamiliar sensation welling up inside of her and she shut it right down. She was not going to cry on the job. Not if she had anything to say about it.

"All right, you two. Get moving. I've got work to do."

It was true, but she knew her mind was going to be mulling over Josephine's words. Sure, she'd stopped the two men from fighting each other, but she was still going to worry what it was like for the little girl to see her dad taken down to the ground by an officer.

Kate knew that image and those words were going to stay in her own head for a long time.

She groaned and went back to the case review she was working on. Two lines into it she blew out a breath and sighed. "I'm going to need a drink tonight."

[5]

ROCK & KATE

It was a slow night at Ciro's, and Kate was happy. Well, not happy, but it made things easier. She wasn't expecting to see Rock. Or maybe the point was, she was hoping that he'd show up after she left.

She wasn't going to hide from him, but she also didn't want things to be awkward or uncomfortable for either one of them.

Yeah, right. Like that was even possible.

Still, she needed a drink to take the edge off. Roan's announcement that their parents were coming for a visit hadn't upset her at first, but knowing that they were expecting to have a big, happy, family dinner to celebrate Roan's engagement was enough to put her in a funk.

Who the hell am I going to blackmail into going with me?

It was a depressing thought. It only got worse when her thoughts turned to Rock.

There was no way that she would take him to a family dinner like that. It was just one step short of taking him as a date to a wedding.

That kind of date would lead to expectations. Not just for Rock but for Cora as well.

She knew her father wouldn't care, but Cora would be dropping hints about biological clocks and nursery school.

Kate just couldn't handle the expectations, because she knew she'd just disappoint everyone, and it would only be a little while until everything would fall apart.

She was a strong woman. Independent. A damn good law enforcement officer, no matter what her captain thought. There were only so many expectations that she could manage at one time.

"Uh, Kate?"

Startled, she turned toward the slightly scratchy tenor voice and saw Patrick watching her carefully.

"Sorry," she sighed. "I've got a few things on my mind."

His soft chuckle wasn't mean, it just was. "I can see that. Anything I can do to help?"

There was something warm and comforting about the bartender. His manner was easy and unassuming most times, but he could also order around drunk assholes when he needed to.

She'd bet a good chunk of money that he would be a good listener. She just wasn't ready to think her thoughts out loud.

"How about a beer."

She'd caught him by surprise.

"Okay!" He grinned at her and his dark eyes brightened. "Any preference? Tap? Bottle?"

She thought she'd make his day. "Surprise me."

He rubbed his hands together with a kind of maniacal glee that almost made her second guess the request.

"You grab a seat, Kate. I'll bring something over to you."

Smiling for the first time since she'd said goodbye to the

officers in the squad room on her way out of the precinct, she started toward one of the empty long tables along the opposite wall.

And then turned back. A lone woman sat at a table with an open book in front of her.

It was an ancient looking romance novel with a cover that was fancy filigree and its title in bright metallic foil.

"What book is that?"

Her head lifted and Kate could see two doe-like eyes behind a pair of bright pink cat-eye frames. For a moment they stared at each other until the bookworm startled and sat up straighter, lowering her book, but not closing it.

"You're asking me, right?"

Kate nodded and smiled. "Yeah. I was curious because it looks like you really like that book."

She lifted a hand to her face and touched her cheek as if she was searching for a smudge of some kind.

Gesturing to the book, Kate lifted her chin. "The spine has been cracked a few times from use. Some cracks deeper than others so I'm guessing that's where the really good stuff is. The cover itself is almost pristine, so you've taken really good care of the book as a whole. It's a favorite. And given how engrossed you were with it when I rudely interrupted you, it's just as good this time as it was the first time."

"Better maybe." The other woman smiled, and Kate could see that her lipstick matched the color of her eyeglass frames. Tucking the book carefully against her chest, she held out a hand. "Irish Healey, book addict."

Kate took her hand in a warm shake. "Kate Turner, Nosy Nellie."

"Well, have a seat, Nosy Nellie." Irish laughed and the sound eased some of the tension in Kate's shoulders. "I haven't heard that phrase in quite some time. I'll have to look up the idiom later."

Kate shook her head. Irish was as unique as they came. "I always associated it with that hateful Nelly Olsen from Little House. If you find out that I'm wrong, let me know."

Irish nodded thoughtfully. "I could see that. Still, her mother was maybe even more nosy. Nellie just liked to talk trash and get in Laura's face."

Kate agreed. "I stand corrected."

Patrick walked over and placed a bottle on a coaster for Kate.

"A relatively new IPA out of Chicago. They advertise a sophisticated and yet substantial flavor. Me? I think it tastes like the best of both worlds."

He gestured for Kate to take a drink. Even as apprehensive as she was to taste it with him watching, Irish leaned against the table with a rapt expression on her face.

"Well," she lifted the bottle up in her hand in almost a toast, "here we go!"

The cold chill of the mouth of the bottle touched her bottom lip and then a moment later, the beer coursed over her tongue and she closed her eyes searching for the name of the flavor that ghosted over her tongue. Startled as a word popped into her head, Kate looked at Patrick. "Coffee?"

He grinned and wagged a finger at her. "You're good! Yeah, don't ask me how they did it, but it's the smoothest blend I've ever tasted."

A customer walked up to the bar with cash in his hand and Patrick excused himself leaving Kate and Irish alone.

Smiling at the other woman, Kate took another sip. "Are you from around here, Irish?"

The look in her eyes shifted a few times, but there was almost a glint of humor. "From? I grew up in Cincinnati, a few hours from here, but I'm guessing that wasn't exactly what you were asking."

Kate shook her head and set her bottle down. "No, but good observation."

Irish's smile twisted up at one side. "I'm currently sharing an apartment with my cousin and his partner on Ambo Sixty-Five."

Kate couldn't help but blurt out a question. "Ambo Sixty-Five? So, he works out of house Twenty-Nine."

"Yeah. Gordon Healey's my cousin." Irish's smile took on a wry twist. "They call him Ramsey."

Kate smacked her hand on the tabletop. "'Cause of his hair, right?"

Irish nodded and her pink tinged curls swished around her head. "You know him?"

Kate shrugged. "Not by his name." Her forehead wrinkled a bit as she thought about her answer. "By the Ambo number. I've been at a few calls where Ambo Sixty-Five was at the scene."

Irish lifted a shoulder in a shrug. "Yeah, I bet. It must be hard having to see all of that up close and personal." She shuddered. "I don't think I could do it."

Kate was still thinking through Irish's earlier words, or lack of them. "You didn't ask me what I was doing there."

Irish blushed a little. "I didn't have to. You're Sergeant Kate Turner! It took me a minute to recognize you without the uniform and updo."

"Uh, okay." Kate sighed. "You saw me on TV, I guess?"

Irish waved it off. "Who hasn't, but you've been an inspiration to me since I moved here. I think I have a stack of interdepartmental bulletins in my desk where you're mentioned. You're a total bad ass in my book!"

Kate was still trying to put the pieces together, and she'd only had a few sips. "Inter-depart-"

Irish's expression turned into a grimace for a moment. "Wow, I must sound like a deranged fan or something."

Kate laughed. After the last few days, she was happy to have a fan.

"I'm sorry. I should have explained that I work in the 911 Call Center. The disembodied voices on the other end of your radios."

Kate nodded. "Our literal lifelines."

Irish looked back at her with a big grin. "That's the best job description!"

Chuckling Kate nodded. "We depend on you guys... girls... women a lot."

Irish was laughing so hard her shoulders shook. "Guys works for me. Just don't call me dude or mister." She waved off the subject.

"You live around here?" Kate felt she could ask the question and not sound like a pickup line.

Irish hesitated. "Gordon's apartment is a few streets over, but believe me, as generous as they've been in letting me use the guest room. I'm seriously looking for a place of my own."

"Oh?" Kate took another sip as her brain started chewing on the idea.

Irish's head bobbled back and forth a little. "It's weird to wake up and see a random woman sneaking out of his bedroom giving me looks like I'm the one who doesn't belong." Irish shook her head and grumbled. "The things I didn't want to know about my cousin."

Kate tried to cover her laugh with a cough. "I'm sorry. But I get it. Have you found a place you're interested in?"

Irish sagged. "There are plenty of great places I can't

afford and plenty of completely horrid places that I'd be afraid to live in. Nothing in the middle."

Kate wasn't usually someone who thought of things as fate, but at that moment in the nearly empty bar, she had a gut feeling that she trusted more than anything else.

"Do you know about a firefighter named Gibson Braun?"

Irish's eyes opened wide.

"Tall and Broad Braun! He works in this area, doesn't he? Damn... what a man."

Kate lost the war to hide her laughter. "I've never heard him called that, but I guess it fits."

Irish blushed almost the same pink as her hair. "I never know when to shut up."

"No worries around me. I've been known to stick my foot in it... a lot."

"Yeah, right." Irish clearly didn't believe her.

"Anyway, Gibson's a carpenter when he's not on shift at Twenty-Nine. And the reason I mentioned him is that he might have an apartment to rent out."

Irish's jaw dropped. "Get out! No way!"

"It's a little more than a block away from here. I rent one of the apartments on the ground floor. One of my officers rents the other one. He's almost ready to rent the two on the second floor. Gibson's offering them at a good price to female first responders in Center City.

Irish leaned closer, against the edge of the table. "I'm not really a first responder, right? You guys are out there with the people making a difference. I sit in a dark room behind a whole wall of computer monitors."

Kate felt a slight pang of pain in her chest that Irish was doubting herself. "You're the first one there at so many calls.

And sometimes it takes time for us to get to a call. You're there, waiting with people in need."

Irish nodded and blinked her eyes as if she was holding back tears. "We try."

Kate gave her an encouraging smile. "Gibson knows what we make since he also works for the city and it's a comfort knowing that we can be there for each other. Helps with security."

Irish winked. "I've got mace and a taser in my purse. So, I can help. I even have my kitty kat keychain."

Kate's brows pinched between her brows. "That's good, I guess."

Irish laughed and reached into her purse. "Here I'll show you."

When her hand reemerged moments later, Kate understood. Irish had slipped her fingers through the keychain like brass knuckles, but instead of a thick metal brace across the top there were two hard metal spikes that looked like stylized kitten ears. "I can see that you've got this down."

Irish smiled and dropped the keychain back into her purse. "You know it!"

Kate knew that Irish was going to be a hell of a friend. "Well, are you interested in checking the place out and talking to Gibson?"

Irish didn't even hesitate. "Of course! Hell yeah!"

Patrick looked up at them from across the room and Kate started laughing. Irish joined in.

That's when Kate noticed who was standing at the bar in front of Patrick.

Rock.

And he looked exhausted.

Some would judge him because his hair was more salt than pepper, but Kate knew that the man standing about twelve feet away had a body that any man would be thrilled to have. Firefighters kept fit because to stay alive they needed body and mind focused and ready. Rock? His body was muscle and hot flesh. And he knew how to use it.

But as he focused on her she could see that he was stressed. His eyes had dark smudges under them, turning his eyes almost a steely gray. He didn't have any of the swagger that she was used to.

She was beginning to wonder if he'd fall over with a good shove.

Kate was up and out of her chair before she realized it. Pausing, she turned back to Irish. "What's your number?"

Irish rattled off her phone number and Kate dialed her phone until Irish's phone peeped like a baby chick. With a smile, Kate ended the call.

"Text me and let me know what your schedule is like. I'll talk to Gibson. Okay?"

Irish looked between Kate and Rock and bit into her lip for a moment before answering. "Yeah, sure. You... have a good night."

Kate mumbled something she hoped was similar and continued across the room. When she reached Rock, she reached out and took hold of his arm. She felt his muscles contract at her touch, but he didn't pull away. He did lower his gaze to her mouth. A muscle ticked in his jaw and she wanted to reach out and touch it.

She didn't trust herself to stop there.

Nor could she move away from him when he looked like he might fall to the floor if she wasn't holding on to him.

"Are you okay?" Kate had no idea why she asked the question. She certainly didn't expect an answer. Rock wasn't just what they called him because of his last name, it was his whole demeanor. He was the rock they could lash themselves to in a storm. The guy who could stand against the current.

They'd never really talked much about the things they'd seen or the things they'd done on the job or in their personal lives.

What they had between them was sex. A way to relieve tension and stress.

Hot? Unbridled? Fuck yeah.

Emotional? Gentle? Loving?

She would rather gargle glass.

Then why was she standing there, her hand on his arm, watching him carefully for any signs that he was weakening?

That he needed her?

And she knew they were being watched.

She was used to living under watchful eyes. Especially the last few days. She'd had enough of it.

Had enough of proving to everyone around her that she was as strong and as badass as she was supposed to be.

And Rock? He looked like he could use a distraction as much as she could.

Kate looked over his shoulder at the door and then lifted her eyes to meet his gaze. "Were you planning to get a drink here?"

"I was planning on… something." He drew in a breath and the rise and fall of his muscled shoulders reminded her of what was underneath that shirt. And the things that he could do with it.

With all of it.

"I might have something you'd like at my place."

His eyes darkened almost to a gunmetal gray and when he swept his tongue over his lower lip, she gave up waiting.

Kate lifted her chin toward the door. "Let's go."

Almost as an afterthought, she turned to Patrick and put her beer bottle in his outstretched hand. "Sorry, Patrick. I promise you. I won't make a habit out of this."

He waved off her apology. "Take good care of my friend Rock and I'll owe you, okay?"

She didn't read into the fact that Rock didn't meet her gaze as she started toward the door. This wasn't about tender feelings or emotions at all, she told herself.

This was about taking his mind off whatever he was worried about.

As the cold air of Center City greeted them outside, Kate stopped and took a good hard look at Rock. He didn't have his usual confident air about him, and she tried to ignore the strange ache she felt. "Unless you tell me no," she let out a long slow breath, "I'm going to take you back to my place and keep you there all night."

The look he gave her was foreign in so many ways. She had no idea what was going on in his head and that scared her a little bit.

"Okay, come on. Let's get you home."

That wasn't what she'd meant to say. Not at all.

But there was no taking it back at that moment.

She doubted he'd remember anything in about an hour. Not after she was done with him.

She tugged on his arm and he went with her.

[6]

ROCK & KATE

He didn't know what made her take him home to her apartment, but he wasn't going to argue. He'd shown up at Ciro's looking for a good stiff drink, but the moment she put her hand on his forearm he'd been good and stiff for a whole lot of other reasons.

And he was hoping to get her hands on them.

Fuck.

Kate always was a take charge kind of woman, but the way she was walking down the street he wouldn't be surprised if she gave him a good swift spank and told him to move faster.

And damn, he wouldn't mind that at all.

Sure, he loved sex, but things had never been as hot or as demanding as Kate Turner could be.

He needed the distraction. Wanted it... wanted her more than his next breath.

It had been a hard day in so many ways. And Seth-

He mentally shook himself. No, while he was with her, he wasn't going to think about the news they'd heard from the hospital. There wasn't anything he could do at the moment anyway. The hospital room and the waiting area nearby was full. He'd only gone to Ciro's to let the staff know what was going on.

And yes, he'd entertained the thought of stopping by Kate's apartment to see if she was in.

This? This was better than he'd hoped for.

He held it all in until she unlocked the door and let him in. Before she even had a chance to lock the door behind them, he had her pressed up against it and his body leaning into her as if she was the only thing holding him up.

And she just might have been.

An indrawn breath felt like his first in the last few hours. Her body felt like heaven against his. Her hips, her belly, felt like they were cradling his dick.

Her breasts?

Heaven help him. He wanted to taste and suck her tits into his mouth. He didn't need a drink when he could have his mouth on her.

"Kate-"

She touched her fingers to his lips, and he stopped talking.

But he didn't stop moving.

He opened his mouth and slowly closed it again, letting his teeth scrape lightly against the pads of her fingers.

"Don't."

Her tone held a command in it, but he felt her hand tremble at his touch.

He nodded and held still.

She kept her gaze focused on him.

"Let me, Rock. Let me take your mind off of whatever happened today. I want to do this for you."

He nodded, slowly. Doing everything he could to keep a physical connection between them.

Maybe it was his imagination.

Or maybe a hallucination.

But he thought he saw her smile.

"Come in the bedroom with me." She slipped out from between him and the door, her movements slow and deliberate.

He wanted to tell her that he was fine right where they were.

He didn't need a bed.

He didn't need a thing, except for her.

And maybe she heard his thoughts because she spoke again.

"Rock? I'm about to pull those jeans down around your knees and I don't want anyone walking by the window to see what I'm going to do to you.

Rock followed her without question and the moment they were inside her bedroom, she did exactly what she said.

Kate reached for him and unhooked the top button on his jeans. It was quick and easy, but the rest of the buttons took a little effort.

He saw her sly smile and knew why. He was already hard, achingly so, and the press of his cock against the front of his jeans made removing the buttons a little more difficult. She didn't complain and when the last button was down, Kate slipped her hand through the opening in his boxers and wrapped her fingers around him.

He almost came right then and there but managed to hold on by clenching the muscles in his jaw hard enough that he might have to worry about a chip.

Kate stepped closer, easing the angle of her arm and as he looked down at the top of her head, he felt her hand draw up to the tip of his cock and back down the length of his shaft, ending when she cupped her palm around his balls.

"Fuck."

He grimaced when he realized that he'd been the one to talk, but it didn't seem to ruin the mood any. She tilted her head to the side and looked up at him. "Later," she winked, "if you're a good boy."

Hell, he'd be good.

As much as he was able.

He'd even fucking wash her car every day of the week and serve her breakfast in bed if it got her to handle him like this.

She drew her hand up again, slower this time, her fingers trailing against the sensitive skin of his sac as she went.

Fuck.

His mind was reduced to that one word. And he had to fight to keep still because he would love to move along with her.

But he knew that's not what she wanted.

Kate wanted to do this to him.

Do this for him.

And he was going to let her...even if it killed him.

Another long stroke and he felt the backs of her fingers brush against his stomach.

Shivers and jolts of sensation pulsed through his skin.

"You like that."

It wasn't a question.

Not that she needed to ask. He was rock hard in her hand.

He felt his dick twitch as she squeezed it, just beneath the head. The sensation was strange, but it wasn't bad. He didn't think she could do anything to him that he wouldn't like. At the very least because it was her.

"Now that I know you like my hand, let's see what happens if I get a little more access.

Her hand withdrew and he felt the loss keenly. His cock was still hard and stiff, but it lost her heat and the cool air of her apartment sent shivers through his body when she pushed his pants down toward his knees.

The look of triumph in her eyes almost undid him.

She threw a look toward the wall. "You might want to lean on that."

Kate didn't wait to see if he'd take her suggestion.

To be honest, he wasn't even sure he'd heard her right, but the instant she lowered herself to her knees in front of him, he had his hand on the wall. His knees suddenly weak.

She leaned forward and brushed her lips over the tip of his cock and when she moved back there was a shiny streak on her upper lip.

Fuck.

Kate leaned forward again and caught the tip of his cock between her gently opened lips as she looked up into his eyes.

Just that touch alone had him on a razor's edge. He didn't have to look to know that his knuckles were white, his fingers curling in his free hand. The hand that wanted to fist in her hair.

It was taking every ounce of his self-control not to push deeper into her mouth, but he was going to let her take the lead.

Oh yeah, she was gonna kill him.

And she came damn close when she leaned toward him and he watched her take him into her mouth, her tongue rubbing the underside of his cock as she went.

Her eyes.

Those beautiful eyes.

She stared up at him as she did it.

His heart thundered in his chest and the muscles in his legs trembled when she swallowed, and her tongue rubbed against him.

Kate reached out and gently trailed her fingers up his thighs, her fingertips brushing against the hair on his legs, making his skin tingle all over.

And then her hand closed around the base of his cock and his knees nearly buckled. "Katie." He was leaning so hard against the wall he was surprised he didn't put a dent in the wood.

Keeping her hand still, she pulled back, and seeing his dick wet from her mouth had him aching, the edges of his vision darkening slightly.

She engulfed him again, her hand squeezing the base of his cock, only to release the slightest bit of pressure when her lips met her fingers.

Rock was lost. "Damn, baby. Fuck me."

Her eyes glared at him for a moment and she pulled back and all the way off of him.

He couldn't stop the groan that fell from his lips or the way his cock bobbed, desperate to get back inside of her.

"Fuck. I'm sorry, Kate. No baby talk."

With a satisfied smile on her lips, she reached out, grabbed the backs of his thighs, and took him in deep.

She didn't pause there, she retreated and pressed forward, devouring him over and over as if she was starving and he was a sweet treat that hit the spot.

And shit yeah, he was hitting something, over and over.

"Ba- Katie, fuck. Oh. Yes. I'm so damn close."

She didn't slow down or pull off of him.

No, Kate Turner only moved faster. And when she started humming and moaning like she was the one about to come, he dropped his free hand to her hair. He didn't try to stop her or control her, he just held on for the ride.

"Kate?" His voice caught in his throat. "If you don't want me to come down your throat," he was gasping for breath, panting as she continued the most amazing blow job he'd ever had, "now's the time to-"

She didn't pull back.

Didn't let him go.

She slipped one of her hands between them and cupped his balls against her calloused palm... and squeezed.

He came apart with a shout and his eyes all but rolled back into his head as Kate drank down everything he gave up.

When all that was left were fluttering twitches in her mouth, she held on with her hand as she let him go with her mouth.

"Shit, Rock." He could hear some humor in her voice and maybe even a soft chuckle. "You're still hard."

Rock looked down and saw the truth of her words. He wasn't fully erect, but he wasn't going to go soft anytime soon. Blood was still coursing through his veins and with her hand on him, it would only continue.

"Think you can come again?" Her eyes were full of mischief and the way her lips pursed reminded him that she'd just had them wrapped around his dick.

"Yeah," he growled. "I think I can if I'm inside you."

"That," she took her hand off of him and reached for the buttons down the front of her blouse, "can be arranged."

When she had opened enough buttons for him to see that she had on her black lace bralette, she tilted her head toward the oversized chair against the wall.

"Sit."

Somehow, he made it there, toeing off his shoes, shaking his jeans off his feet. He shoved his boxers down and heard a rip just before they fell away. He didn't care.

"Don't forget the shirt."

His teeth ground together as he pulled his t-shirt up and off his body, dropping it on the floor as he sat back in the chair. The cushion was firm beneath him, his arms loose at his sides. Rock couldn't seem to do anything else but stare at Kate as she dropped her blouse on the bed and made quick work of her jeans. When she stepped into him, nudging his legs further apart with her own, she hooked her thumbs into the waist of her lacy boy shorts and wiggled them off her hips.

With her hair back he got a delicious look at her tits as she bent over, and on the way back up, she grabbed a hold of his thigh to brace herself.

His dick liked that.

A lot.

And Kate? She didn't miss a thing. Her eyes fixed on him before she licked her lips.

He groaned.

It was all he could do.

"If you take me in your mouth again, I just might die from the pleasure."

She dragged her gaze away from his erection and met his eyes in a wild challenge. "Don't say things like that if you don't want me to see if it's possible."

"Murder by orgasm?" He shrugged and smiled from ear to ear. "I'd be okay with that."

"Well," she sighed, and put one knee outside of his thigh, "I don't want to kill you."

It seemed a little disingenuous of her. Placing her knee

where she had left her legs open enough for him to see the curls on her mons. He could only hope she planned on letting him in or maybe she was going to tease him until he passed out.

Either way, he'd go happy.

When she leaned forward and braced her hands on his shoulders, he tensed up all over.

She straddled his thighs and leaned even closer, cheek to cheek, so she could whisper into his ear. "I can't wait to feel you inside me."

That's all that it took for him to swallow his own tongue and lose all powers of speech.

Kate Turner was going to ride him.

His cock had never been so hard or so hungry.

He couldn't even control his hands as they reached for her and grabbed a hold of her ass. That perfect ass. His palms cupped her lovingly, but his fingers dug in and pulled her flush against his cock.

She didn't argue or push his hands away.

That might have saved his sanity.

Instead, Kate kept one hand in place, and as she leaned back, she used the other hand to pull the lacy cup of lingerie off to the side, baring her breast.

He stopped breathing when she drew a fingertip over her areola. Her nipple pebbled tighter in its wake.

"I think," she repeated the gesture with a sigh, "I want to feel your tongue on me." She pinched her nipple between her fingers and arched against him. "Right now."

His hands left her ass and took hold of her ribs, lifting her higher. He was a strong man by nature. He kept fit because it helped save lives, his own included, but it also helped him at moments like this. Rock leaned down and swept his tongue over the tip of her breast, loving the breathless gasp from her lips.

He did it again and she squirmed against him.

And the third time, he ended it by closing his teeth on her sensitive skin.

"Yes."

Her head fell back, pushing her breast against his mouth, and he suckled on her.

"Oh god!" One of her hands clung to the back of his head, holding him tighter.

He turned his head and let his beard brush against her swollen skin, and she ground her hips against him.

In one moment of clarity, he thanked fate for the fact that they'd both had a physical right before he'd bumped into her the first time at a fundraiser for Cole Medical's Clinic. From that first time they'd gone without condoms saving so much time and making everything between them that much more amazing.

When he took her nipple back into his mouth and swirled his tongue around it, she grabbed onto the back of his head again with both hands. He couldn't really hear the words coming out of her mouth, but he didn't really care. He heard the heat in her voice, the desperation in her short pants of breath.

His fingers pulled aside the other delicate piece of black lace and he teased her other breast the way he'd done her first.

Before he finished, she lowered her hands back to his shoulders and her body onto his cock.

He'd never felt her so wet.

Kate's pussy slid down over him, gripping him just as tight as her hand had done earlier. With the way it was pulsing around him, he had a feeling she was really close to coming.

He wasn't sure what she had in mind, but he was there for all of it.

"Kate."

She pressed her nipple back against his lips, making a mindless mewling sound.

"Kate? Do you want me to move?" Just the thought had him lifting his hips up from the chair and fitting them even closer together. "Do you want me to fuck you?"

She shook her head and her body moved against him. "N... no. No... don't."

She braced her hands on his shoulders again and that was the end of their conversation.

Kate Turner turned him inside and out. She rode him, hard. She moved like she was losing her own mind and taking him with her. He just had to hold on.

He held onto her hips. Her ass. Her breasts.

He touched her as she touched him, only he was sure that she didn't know he was all in with her. Rock knew he'd find some way to tell her later, but there was no way he was going to interrupt when he was dangerously close to losing himself inside of her for the second time that night.

All he could do was hope to bring her along with him. This was not something he wanted to do alone.

Reaching his hand down between them, he slipped his thumb through her curls and wiggled it until he felt the swollen nub of her clitoris.

He swore he could feel it pulse against his fingertip and that only made him press harder. He stroked her higher and higher and as he felt his balls pull up tight, his whole body tensed, with one last rub she went over the edge.

Fuck. Kate Turner owned him.

Her body sucked at his, bathed him with her release. There was no way to really explain what he felt or what happened in those few transcendent moments besides the world turning upside down and taking them both for a ride.

When she finally collapsed against his chest, he was too spent to lift them up and move to the bed, so he just wrapped his arms around her and held her until she was fast asleep with his cock softening inside of her.

He wanted this and so much more with her.

She might not want a relationship and he would work with that, but he knew he wanted her.

So, he laid his head back against the cushion of her chair and fell asleep with her held securely in his embrace.

[7]

ROCK & KATE

Kate gradually came awake, stretching slowly under the covers. What a night!

With a languid sigh and a broad smile curving her lips, she turned over and reached for Rock.

The half of the bed closest to the wall was empty. The sheets and pillow cool to the touch. She wanted to pull the pillow closer, but she pushed that thought away before she could act on it.

He was gone.

That was good, right?

Those were the rules.

She had nothing to complain about.

Reaching behind her she slapped her hand on the nightstand and almost sent her phone skidding to the floor.

"Just fucking great." Sitting up she let her blanket fall to her waist. Turning on her phone she opened her texts and stared at the screen. No new texts. "Okay." Switching to the phone she touched Rock's number and sat there, staring at it.

She could call, but it was early. Too early to be polite.

Fuck polite!

But she stopped herself.

He left.

He was probably sleeping.

And waking him up at this hour was a dick move.

And she... to be honest? She wanted his dick.

No. Well, yeah. But she kind of thought that this morning might be different.

Or that they could talk about things.

She was curious about his mood when she saw him at the bar. Sure, she didn't talk about it when she brought him home. She didn't think he wanted to talk. At least he hadn't complained when she'd been on her knees.

And on his lap.

Finally, in bed, when she'd faced him and lightly scratched her fingers through his beard, she started to ask him what had happened.

He'd cut her off with a kiss.

Kate couldn't help the smile that touched her lips when she remembered how hard it was to talk with his tongue in her mouth.

She wanted him again.

And she had no idea where he was.

Throwing back her sheet, she dropped her feet to the floor and stood. A quick search of a drawer had her dressed in no time. All she needed were socks and sneakers and she was off, tucking her small key chain into the pocket on her hoodie.

It was O-Dark-Whatever, but there were lights enough to run, and while Genevieve Gardens wasn't really lit in the wee hours of the morning, there would be enough ambient lighting from Cole Medical Center that she could see where she was going.

The cold was bracing and if she wasn't careful, she'd catch a chill, or slip on some snow or ice. But no matter what, it was better than moping around waiting to hear from Rock.

Jogging down Thirtieth Street, she put a foot in a puddle of slush and uttered a curse, telling herself, "See? This is why I don't need to get serious."

Her mother had. She'd met, dated, and married Kate's father. And then he'd gone off, screwed his secretary and a few other women and left her mother crying herself to sleep for months.

If you don't care, you don't get hurt.

A flash of lights and the short blast of a car horn had Kate jumping back and out of the way.

She didn't stop to think about it, she barely had time to see the cab driver flash her the bird, she just kept on running.

Rock looked up as Aldo Campanelli walked into the waiting room with Doctor Callen Webb. From somewhere off to his side, Rock saw his friend Russell get up on his feet ahead of everyone else. It wasn't just that Russell was worried about Seth, Doctor Webb was his father and the two hadn't managed to come to terms with the fact that Russell had joined the Center City Fire Department instead of going to college and then medical school.

Aldo looked over the assembled group and Rock could

see the strain in their Chief's face. He looked much older than his real age and bone tired.

"I know you're all concerned for Seth and he would be so happy to know that you all came down at a moment's notice to be here for him, but you should go home."

Predictably, the group began to talk, but Rock easily picked out Faust's voice. Isaac had the closest relationship to Seth, and they would all let him speak first.

"What's happening right now?" As the question stilled the other voices and settled a few back into their chairs, Rock could see Faust easily at the heart of their group. "I'm sure we've all heard some conflicting information and I know I wasn't in any condition to understand all of the jargon that was thrown around when they asked us to leave his room."

Leaning into his shoulder, Vitalia squeezed his arm to comfort him even though she was likely just as worried as Faust was.

It was quiet enough in the waiting area for Rock to hear her whisper to his lieutenant. "It's going to be okay..."

Doctor Webb gestured toward the hall. "Mister Mackenzie, if you'd like to step into the hallway, I can tell you more. You are his Medical Power of Attorney and I can tell-"

"You can tell everyone, Doctor."

Rock heard the rough scratch of Faust's voice and knew what he was saying was true.

"At Station Twenty-Nine, we're a family. There's very little we don't know about each other and Seth would be more than fine with you telling us all what's happening. If you don't, I'll be sharing it with them and I'm probably going to get it all wrong."

Doctor Webb looked at Aldo and they all saw Aldo nod in reply. Shaking his head, the doctor let out a sigh and looked at the folder in his hand. He didn't open it. He had been looking in on Seth every day since he'd been admitted and likely knew his condition in a more concrete way than the words scribbled into his file. "The infection that we've been watching has become... more aggressive in the last few hours. We've had to take some measures to excise the damaged muscle in his thigh."

Faust swayed on his feet and Vitalia wrapped her arms around his middle, holding him steady.

"We have a PICC line inserted and the antibiotics that we're giving him are our best chance of clearing out the infection fast enough... Look, we're going to do everything we can to get this infection under control, so we don't have to take him back into surgery."

Rock wanted to say that the words were comforting, but they weren't.

He'd woken up in Kate's bed when his phone reacted to an incoming call. He'd had the good sense to turn off the ringer, but he'd left it on vibrate and the damn phone vibrated its way right off of the nightstand and onto the floor.

It had been Vitalia's name and picture that was on the screen and he'd answered immediately, taking the phone into Kate's bathroom to let her sleep in peace.

Hearing the news, or rather what he could understand through Vitalia's panicked tones, he knew he had to get to the hospital.

There was a moment when he considered waking Kate up and telling her what was going on, but she was so damn peaceful that he knew he couldn't wake her. With all the crap going on at work and the continuing bad press surrounding the domestic call that she'd gone to... he just couldn't disturb her like that.

He'd sent her a quick text to say he'd gone to see Seth and hoped that she'd understand what he meant. Later, when he was sure she'd be up, he'd call her and apologize.

Sure, they'd agreed to keep the sex casual and no-strings, but he wasn't going to be rude.

She'd let him into her apartment and taken the edge off of all the worry about Seth and when she'd gone further and tried to talk to him about it, he'd silenced her with his tongue and then eaten her to another orgasm before they'd fallen asleep in her bed.

Now that the group was starting to disperse, he pulled out his phone and looked at the time.

Shit. It was way too early to call her.

Hell, it was way too early to do much of anything.

Faust sent him a look that had him on his feet. Most of the Station Twenty-Nine folks were slowly making their way out of the waiting room, but the Rescue Crew were going to talk for a bit. They would likely set up shifts to stay with Seth. Even though he was unconscious and not likely to wake anytime soon, they'd watch over him in case the family needed to be called back. He was one of their crew and Rock was only too happy to help.

Putting his phone away, Rock walked over and dropped a kiss on Vitalia's head. She might not be a firefighter at Twenty-Nine, but she was family in more ways than one. Even if Faust had his head in the sand when it came to her.

Kate finished giving out the assignments to her officers before heading down to the desk to start another shift of her punishment. Sure, no one called it that out loud, but it was what it was.

Desk duty was like being benched on a sports team. You got to watch things going on around you, but there wasn't much you could do in your own capacity.

She would put all of her effort in for her people and she'd be happy to do whatever she was assigned to do. Not because she enjoyed the activity or the busy work, but because she expected the best from her officers, so she'd give her best and serve as an example.

And this morning she was ready to face the world and the curious stares she got from her fellow officers.

"Turner?"

Looking toward the source of the sound, she saw Captain Catalano standing in nearly the center of the room, his hands at his sides and a stern look on his face.

"I need you to come to my office."

He lifted his chin and flicked his gaze toward the ceiling over her head. It was an unnecessary gesture. She knew where his office was.

Everyone else in the room knew where his office was too.

And they all likely knew that she'd been upstairs just moments before, speaking to her officers. The Captain could have easily grabbed her up there after the roll call or mentioned something beforehand. Then she would have gone to his office just as quietly, but also without transforming those curious looks to downright worry or glee.

Yes, she had spent the better part of five years working for the CCPD after taking a lateral step from Chicago, and she'd made quite a few friends on the force in Center City, but now was the time when she learned that a number of those officers would just as soon watch her fall as those who would celebrate her success.

She didn't give them much time to stare.

As soon as the captain headed for the elevator, she took the stairs and used every single step to pound some calm into her head. It wasn't going to work with her heart, that was going to keep pounding until it wasn't. There was no need to hide from the captain. Whatever he was going to say was just that, decided. She just had to hear it.

Entering his office, she saw him sit down behind his desk and lean back into the plush desk chair that he was famous for: perfect, buttery leather that shone just as much as the polished surface of his desk.

"Close the door and have a seat."

She closed the door all right, but when she turned back, she lifted her chin the slightest bit. "I'd prefer to stand, sir."

Captain Catalano nodded. "I'll make this quick."

Fuck.

The Captain settled his weight on one arm of his chair. The room was so quiet, Kate heard the metal creak.

"Doug Fitchett, the man you restrained, has filed a lawsuit against you and the CCPD."

Her skin went cold, clammy, and her chest felt empty as if her heart had fallen out of her chest.

Captain Catalano went on talking for a few minutes, but all she heard in the midst of the ringing in her ears was 'administrative leave' and 'go home.'

Like a robot, she pulled her sidearm from her holster, directing it to the cement wall as she cleared the weapon. She set it on the desk, feeling the echo of the heavy sound pass through her body. Her shield was next, and it almost killed her.

Once it was down on the desk, she gave it one last look before leaving the room.

Pilar and her regular partner, Crois St. Cyr, looked up as she entered the squad room. She didn't have it in her to ask them why they were still there. Knowing them, they'd turned back from the parking lot when word of the Captain's summons reached their ears.

There really weren't a whole lot of secrets even in a police force the size of Center City's. She looked at them but didn't meet their eyes. "I'm headed home. I'm sure the Captain will assign you a new Sergeant for... for the time being. Just do your jobs and you'll be fine. If you could let the others know, I would be grateful for your help."

She'd started to move then, determined to get out of the precinct with as much of her dignity intact as was humanly possible.

Kate nearly lost it a moment later when Pilar and Crois caught up to her and Pilar touched her arm.

"What's going on?"

Kate swallowed and pulled herself together. "I'm sure you'll hear about it anyway. This is just snowballing out of control. Doug Fitchett is suing me and the department. I'm sure they'll be serving me papers later today, but the Captain already let me know."

Pilar's sharp eyes didn't miss a thing. "He took your badge and gun?"

Thank heavens she'd kept her voice down. "I'm on my way home. You two," her tone was pointed even if her voice wavered as well, "have work to do. Watch out for each other."

Crois, normally a mix of growly and snarky, gave her a

look of concern that nearly did her in. "Always, Sarge. But we'll be watching out for you, too. Would you mind if I stop by later and bring you something to eat?"

Her shoulders slumped a little and she managed a smile as she shook her head. "I'm okay, Crois, but thanks. I'll be fine. Now go. I'm going to stay in tonight and put my feet up."

She waited for them to leave and then realized that they weren't going to give up so easily. Lifting her hand, she made a little 'shooing' gesture. "Go on now! Protect and Serve, hmm?"

That said, she turned and walked away.

She was still hurting inside as if she'd gone a few rounds with Attila the Hun, but there was a hint of a smile on her face.

She had friends. Good ones. And she would hold onto that as long as she could.

She made it all the way to her door before her phone rang again.

Kate didn't even have to look before she answered. There was only one number on her contact list that had the ringer set for the original General Hospital theme song. Shouldering open her door she brought the phone up to her ear. "Pilar called you."

She heard his soft laughter through the connection.

"She's worried about you. So am I."

"Hey," she locked the door behind her and tossed her keys on the kitchen counter, not bothering to hang it up on the hook inside the door, "I'm fine. This will blow over."

"Kate, I love you, but I'm not buying it. The man is suing you!"

"It's the nature of-"

"Stop. Just stop!"

Kate was shaken. She wasn't used to that tone of voice coming from Roan. Walker, sure, but he was the brother who had no problem telling her where to step off. Even when she was right. But Roan?

"Kate, please, just listen to me, okay?"

"Yeah," she blinked back the tears that threatened to blur her vision, "I'm listening."

She heard his soft sigh. "I've called an attorney."

Kate bit into her lower lip to keep from arguing with him.

"I know what you're thinking. You're going to tell me that you have an attorney through the union." She smiled. He had her pegged. "Pilar says the Department is being sued too. Do you really trust them to do right by you?"

A cold chill moved through her body. She hadn't thought about that. When it came down to it, there was going to be a lot of money involved in a civil lawsuit. Who would they really put their effort into representing when it came down to the brass tacks?

"Okay, I see your point, Roan. Thanks."

"I've already given her a retainer fee for you and your phone number."

She started to argue and somehow, he knew what she was up to.

"Don't argue, Kate. You've got to feel like everything's coming at you like a freight train. Let me help you. Let me be there for you."

Kate sagged against the door, her chin dropping to her chest as she fought off tears. "Okay. Okay."

"I love you, Kate. You're the best sister I've ever had."

"You're the best brother I've ever had." She grinned even as tears gathered on her lashes.

"You know," Roan sighed, "one of these days I have to record that and play it for Walker."

"Ha. Ha."

"Hey. My break is over, but I'm here if you need me."

"Seriously, Roan. I appreciate it, but tonight I need some alone time."

"I get it."

Kate's phone pinged and she looked down. It was a text from Roan.

"That's the attorney's name, email, and phone number. Oh, I'll send you a picture too. Better safe than sorry. Meet with her. And we'll get through this. Love you."

"Love you."

She hung up after that. Kate couldn't trust herself not to dissolve in a teary, sappy mess. The very thought gave her hives.

Looking down at herself, she saw the all too familiar CCPD uniform and had to fight back the sudden stab of anger at the position she was in. She believed in herself and believed that what she'd done had been appropriate, but she really couldn't control how other people saw her actions. If the CCPD was going to throw her under the bus, she had no idea what was going to happen after that.

Kate started to undo the buttons down the front of her uniform shirt while walking into her bedroom. A shower wasn't necessary, but it would feel damn good. She was almost to the door of the bathroom when there was knock at her door.

It wasn't Gibson. He'd just call through the window, rattling the glass.

It wasn't Pilar; she was still on patrol and she had her own key.

It certainly wasn't Rock. She was fairly sure she'd ruined that somehow and-

The knock sounded again, and Kate had a sudden knot form in her belly. It was probably the person serving her the lawsuit papers.

She shrugged. Better sooner than later.

Pressing her uniform top closed, she crossed to the front door, her steps slowing slightly as she saw who was standing on her doorstep.

Kate opened the door with a rueful smile. "I didn't expect to see you here."

[8]
ROCK & KATE

Talk about quick. Serena Campos, the lawyer who Roan had told her about was standing on her doorstep, looking like she walked right off the cover of an upscale style magazine. She looked more like a model than an attorney.

Then again, Kate cautioned herself, what did she know about what lawyers wore, anyway?

Kate looked down and put her hand over her heart to hold her uniform shirt together. "I'm sorry, I was just about... never mind. Do you want to come in?" She gestured toward the table and chairs next to the kitchenette.

Smiling, the other woman stepped inside, but waited to walk to the table until Kate shut and locked the door. "I'm sorry for showing up unannounced, but Roan made it sound extremely time sensitive."

Standing there, stunned, Kate didn't know what to say or do. "Honestly, I'm at a loss. I've had minor issues on calls before, but I've never faced something like this. Not ever." She gestured to the refrigerator. "I'm sorry, can I get you something to drink?"

Serena shook her head. "Please, Kate, sit down. I'm not here to make you worry about things in your own home. I want to see what I can do to help you."

"Thanks." Kate sank into a chair and sighed. "What do we do first?"

Looking at the notepad she'd set down, Serena started from the top. "Do you have a copy of the filing?"

Kate's shoulders sagged a little. "I didn't think to ask for a copy at the station and when you knocked, at first I thought it was someone coming to serve me with the papers."

Nodding, Serena reached down into her bag and pulled out a small folder. She flipped through the papers quickly and then set a form in front of Kate before laying a pen down beside it.

"This is just a formality. I have the retainer check of Roan-"

"Busybody brother," Kate grumbled grudgingly under her breath. "I love him so much."

"I just need you to sign this form saying that you're designating me as your attorney of record. This way I can go down to the courthouse and pull all the paperwork I need to. No big deal."

Kate blew out a breath that lifted a few errant hairs from her forehead into the air. "Good to know."

The two women chuckled as Kate finished signing and pushed the paper back to Serena.

Looking it over to make sure it was all signed and dated in the right places, Serena put the paper into her folder and set it aside. "Okay, now I'd like to ask you some basic questions about the case."

Kate nodded. "Trying to make sure I've got my story straight?"

Serena's wince told her that her words hadn't come across the right way.

"Sorry, Roan tells me I have a gallows sense of humor."

"And your brother would be right. If this ever gets to court, we're going to have to work on that in witness prep, but for now, let's just move on."

Kate's mind, what was left of it, latched on to a few of Serena's words. "If this goes to court? So, there's a chance that he might drop the suit?"

Serena wiggled in her seat. "I doubt that's going to happen unless we discover something really compelling that we can take to a judge. Or if something else happens that changes the narrative."

"Narrative, huh? I was never really big on my English classes. I'll try to keep my attention focused, looking for something to change the narrative. Gotcha." She cursed under her breath. "This is all a nightmare, you know?"

Nodding, Serena sympathized. "I totally understand. When it's things like Civil Lawsuits, sometimes it's just a crazy random thing that happens and people don't even know it's coming."

"I certainly felt blindsided today." She swallowed and flinched as her throat scratched a little. "Uh, I'm going to need some water. You?"

"Sure thanks," Serena answered. "That'll be good. And here you are. An officer with the CCPD. A clean record. A woman, sorry, officer who cares about her town and the people in it. And suddenly, it's got to feel like the world is closing in and the people are piling on. It's never an easy feeling like you've done the right thing and you're going to be punished for it."

Kate felt an ache bloom in her chest. "I don't think of it like that."

Serena's pen stilled and she looked up. "Then how do you think about it?"

Kate shrugged and yet she still struggled with the words. "I saw that little girl as those two men headed for each other like freight trains. I never was good at those math questions about when a train would reach its destination and all that. But I've trained for this kind of physical assault. I know the kind of damage a body can do to another.

"I can read facial expressions. Body language too. Her step-father was trying to stop her father."

"And her father?" Serena's voice was a little hushed. "What was he trying to do?"

Kate didn't want to picture it in her head, but up it came. The tight clench of the man's jaw. The bone-white of his knuckles. The bunched muscles under his skin. But the image in her mind that still scared her... were his eyes.

"He was going to kill someone." Kate let a breath into her lungs slowly and held it for a moment before she let it out.

"What did you feel? How did you feel when you realized that?"

"Scared."

Serena's voice was softer than before. "Scared?"

Kate nodded, feeling her heart stutter in her chest. "I had adrenaline to push me through at that moment, but whenever it's a domestic case like this... especially when children are involved, people do things they wouldn't do on any other day. Whatever had come before that moment had boiled over. I haven't had a chance to look at the investigation into their past because I'm involved in it, but that day was a tipping point of some sort. When I made the decision to subdue him, it was done for the simple reason that if I could stop his aggression toward her stepfather there was a chance to resolve this without someone being critically injured and traumatized even more."

"I saw the video, Kate. And I watched it a few times after Roan called me."

Her expression was open and calm. Kate didn't see any disappointment or judgment in her dark eyes.

"That man had to have more than fifty pounds on you."

"Almost a hundred." The words came out before Kate could stop herself.

"Did you worry that you wouldn't be able to stop him?"

Kate half-shrugged. "Stop? No. Momentum was always going to be the problem. So, I couldn't stop him, not physically. He could have blown through me like a tornado through a double-wide. The point of what I was doing was to deflect and then subdue.

"If I could knock him off the trajectory that he was on, there was a chance that his rush of energy would fade or burn out. I couldn't bring him to his knees by standing in his way, so I went for smarter, not harder.

"One of the top reasons why people don't think women police officers can handle things like this is that some women, no judgement mind you, try to power through things. They feel like they have to fight them in the gym, like hand-to-hand combat. And some of those moves are helpful. Knowing what they're about to do is key.

"Angry controlling men are steam trains. They're not thinking, so WE have to think, be strategic."

Serena continued on that strategic path and less than an hour later, Kate felt like she'd just faced a battery of reporters at a press conference with the network news shows.

Wrung out.

Rode hard and put up wet.

None of those phrases really put a pin in the idea that she'd been struggling with most of the day, so she pushed the idea to the back of her head. Serena really was trying to help her, and Kate felt like she was going to be the perfect person to guide her through this mess. Deciding to come a little clean, Kate looked across the table at her.

"I hope I don't seem rude or ungrateful. I'm still stunned. I wasn't even going to contact a lawyer on my own. I was going to call my union rep tomorrow."

Serena shook her head. "I'm sure Roan explained why he called me instead. I agree with him. You're the low hanging fruit if you'll excuse the phrase." She cleared her throat. "The higher ups are going to look to protect the CCPD. They don't want the negative press. Sure, you're a good officer. A great one if I want to admit looking up your record for myself the other day."

That shocked Kate but she didn't say anything.

"You have always had an exemplary record as an officer. High marks all the way through the academy. And yet you haven't sought to climb up higher than sergeant."

Kate let out a pent-up breath. "Roan and I talked about this the other day and I think he was right." She rushed on to say, "Just please don't tell him I said that."

"Attorney client privilege." Serena lifted a hand to her mouth and made an X over it. "What did you two discuss?"

Kate shrugged. "A few things." She hedged and then decided just to tell her. "But basically, he thinks I'm like a mama bear to my officers. At first, I laughed it off. If these were my kids, they're 'big' kids. And sometimes they act like it.

"And then there are times I would be more than happy to put them up for adoption, but I want to protect them. Not just in the idea that I'd take a bullet for them, that goes without saying, but I'm also there to help them make better decisions. Be better officers.

"Maybe that's why this is hitting me so hard, you know?" Kate blinked away a new rush of tears. "How can I be an example to them if I'm being accused of this... of this kind of... I can't!"

Serena gently took hold of her forearm and lowered it to the table, her eyes fixed on Kate's face. "That's just it. This is exactly why you fight this. You did what you were trained to do. You got him to stop. You prevented him from doing bodily harm to someone else. His daughter didn't have to see him physically fight her stepfather. No blood was shed, and that little girl got to see a police officer do what they swore to do. Protect."

Kate wanted to grasp onto the feeling of hope that was starting to well up inside. "I've been trying to ignore all the things in the press. All the things online-"

"And you need to. You really do need to ignore all of that. I've got a tech guru who already has keyword searches looking for any useful information on the situation. YOU," she gave Kate's arm a gentle shake, "stay away from the crazy."

"I think I live in the crazy sometimes. Being in law enforcement isn't easy. We have officers who were born and raised in the stone ages where it was fine to get a little rough because they wore the badge."

Serena nodded. "And I'm sure they're also the guys that call you sweetheart and dearie and look down their noses at the sight of you carrying a badge and a gun."

Kate's smile was instinctual. "Exactly."

Smiling in return, Serena gave Kate's arm a gentle pat. "Same thing in a law practice. Every once in a while, I see a few of the guys catch themselves before they say something really stupid."

"But I'm sure stupid happens all the time." Kate was beginning to understand Serena quite a bit.

"Especially when I was working for a law firm here in the city. Sometimes, in a meeting, one of the senior partners would ask me to repeat what someone said. That's when I would turn to the guy taking down the notes for us. I'm not a secretary. I have a law degree from a better school than a few of my old bosses, but I couldn't remind them of that because they'd say I was too sensitive, or prickly.

"Then again, the day I quit my old firm," her expression softened, but the corners of her mouth turned up in a bigger smile. "Old Mister Sanders reached over after the court had excused everyone so the judge could go to his chambers. He pinched me on the cheek and asked me to go get him a cup of coffee while we were waiting for the judge to call us back.

"I'm fairly sure that my face was redder than my mama's rojo sauce, but I prepared to grind my teeth together and let it go."

Kate winced knowing that it wasn't going to end there.

"Then he told me, in a voice loud enough to reach the other side of the room. 'You know, you look so much better when you smile, right?'"

Kate's chin dropped and her mouth just sat there, open and stunned.

"You know, the thoughts that I had in that moment weren't worth losing my law license over, and I had grand plans for my career. So, I packed up my things and walked out of the courtroom. I tendered my letter of resignation the next day and found a small office space to rent.

"If I'm going to practice law the way I want, then I am going to root for people who deserve it."

Kate let out a pent-up breath and relaxed a little. "That's why I went into Law Enforcement. I wanted to stand up for people and help them. I wanted to be on the side of the people, protecting them." After another breath, Kate posited a question. "Do you mind if I ask how you and Roan know each other?"

Serena shook her head. "It's no big secret. I had a client who was injured in a DUI hit and run accident. Months after the crash, my client found out that he'd never walk again and then, adding insult to injury, the drunk driver turned around to sue *my* client! Well, I've worked in some areas where you're lucky to just get a few scribbled notes in a chart. I went to see your brother at the ER and asked him for the records for my client on that night. Well, I got more than I'd asked for. Looking at his notes was also eye-opening. He's got the nicest doctor handwriting I've ever seen. Does that come from your side of the family?"

Serena must have seen Kate flinch at the question, hesitating before speaking again. "Did I say something wrong?"

"Not really," Kate half-shrugged, "we're step-sibs."

"Ahh... got it."

"Seriously though, I've had doctors and whole medical systems refuse me even when I hand them the release form for the information. Your brother was not only gracious, but he was a font of information and it made all of the difference. With his testimony on the stand, we were able to get my client a settlement that covered his care and therapy. It meant so much to me that Roan did that.

"So, when he called me about this case, I was only too happy to help. But I want to tell you something, Kate."

Anticipation wasn't her friend. Kate heard the words Serena was saying and her whole body tensed up. She just wasn't ready for the gently reassuring tone of Serena's voice.

"We're not going to stop." She offered a smile. "We're going to walk through this like it's one of those obstacle courses, over sawhorses, under barbed wire. You and me. Okay? What we're not going to do is stop and give up."

Kate's mind finally caught up with her heart and she nodded slowly. "Okay. I get it."

Serena sat back in her chair and gave Kate a big, broad smile. "Then we're on the same page and I can work with that."

Kate leaned forward and felt a modicum of her humor returning. "I just have a quick question about this obstacle course."

Her expression sobering, Serena met Kate's eyes with an open look. "Okay."

"Are you going to wear those shoes? I don't think we're going to get far in the mud with those things on your feet."

Serena looked down at her dark purple heels that matched her fitted coat. She sat back up and shrugged with a wry smile on her face. "If I need to, I'll kick them off."

Kate reached her hand across the table and Serena gave it a good, solid shake. "Let's do this."

By the time the doctors could give them a solid answer on Seth's prognosis, Rock felt like he'd aged a good decade. As he stood, hunched over one of the sinks in the restroom, cold water dripping off his nose and forehead, he was pretty sure that if he just leaned over a little further and touched the top of his head to the wall, he could fall asleep right there.

When the door opened up behind him, Rock didn't

even bother to look and see who it was. He just wiped the arm of his shirt over his face to get off the rest of the water.

"Rock?"

Stretching his back, as he stood up straight, Rock met Roan's eyes in the wall-sized mirror. "Roan. How are you?"

He couldn't quite understand the look on the other man's face.

"Something wrong?"

Roan's eyes narrowed at him as he turned his body to lean his hip against the sink. "Me? No, but I'm surprised to see you here."

Rock didn't know why but the doctor's answer pricked his temper. "Why? I've been here since... since before dawn."

The eyes that fixed on his face weren't those of a doctor. They were the sharp, disappointed look of a brother. "I get it." Roan turned toward the door and Rock got there before he did. His hand slammed against the edge of the door where it met the frame. Both looked down at the pull bar before they met each other's eyes, tension simmering in the air.

"You. Get. What?"

Roan shrugged. "Your friend is sick. I'm glad you were here for him. I spoke to Callen. Looks like Seth is out of danger."

Rock nodded, but still had his eyes fixed on the younger man. "That's what they just told us, but not what you're upset about."

"You know," Roan's shoulders dropped as he shook his head, "Kate told me that you two weren't a thing. I thought she was totally trying to blow smoke right up my ass. And I'd have believed it if it was Walker talking. He'll never find someone to settle down with. I just thought the two of you were hiding it."

A frustrated huff of air blew past Rock's lips. "Is this like that doctor thing?" He didn't even wait for Roan to try to answer. "Instead of writing illegible crap in a file you're just talking in circles... for what? You don't like what Kate and I do?" Rock took his hand down off the door and walked back to get another paper towel. "What we do... it works okay? And if you're trying to tell me that I need to get on the ball and put a ring on her finger... well, that's good. You're a good brother. But you don't need to do that."

It gave him a little measure of satisfaction that Roan looked a little taken aback by his words.

"I don't need to tell you to make an honest woman of my sister? Well, great. I wasn't planning to. I just thought that with all of the times you seem to find your way into her bed that maybe, along the way, you might have developed some feelings for her that go beyond getting yourself off when you want to."

The room went silent and neither of them moved or said a thing, until a single droplet of water fell from the faucet to the metal bowl beneath.

"You think I don't care about her beyond fucking?"

A muscle ticked in Roan's jaw. "I'd have chosen different words to say it." He nodded. "At least out loud, but yeah. I know Seth is close to you. And you all care for each other like family. That's good. He's lucky to have that. My question is... why you're not over at Kate's right now."

"Kate?" Rock lifted a hand and put some direct pressure on his temples. He was going to have a headache soon with all of the fluorescent lights and stress. "What's wrong with her?"

The look on Roan's face changed again. The anger bled

out of it and was replaced with confusion and more than a trace of sadness.

"She was put on administrative leave today. Captain Catalano took her badge and sidearm. Sent her home. The man she subdued is suing her and the department for some dumb ass reason. Hey-"

The door swung shut on Roan's protest, but Rock didn't fucking care.

Kate had all but lost her job. She was being sued by that piece of shit asshole. And he didn't know a thing about it?

"Fuck, baby. You should've called me." He grumbled under his breath as if he had to hide the words from her, but that wasn't the case. She would have given him a dirty look for the 'baby' part of it anyway. He just couldn't understand why she didn't call him or at least text?

He headed for the double doors that lead to the parking lot and almost ran straight into Greco and Mats.

"Where's the fire, Rock?"

The urge to flip off Nikolas was strong, but he didn't have time to push back at the man. "I've got a family emergency to take care of. Can you let Faust or Vitalia know?"

Mats was the one who reacted first. "Family? You got family in town, Rock?"

He was already crossing the lane into the public parking area and didn't have time to shoot the shit with his friends.

Family. The word had rolled off of his tongue too easily.

Kate? Family?

Of course, she was.

You don't love someone like your next breath and not think of them as part of the fabric of your very existence. Maybe other people felt that way, but he didn't. He was going to talk to Kate and find out how they were going to get through this. It didn't matter how much she tried to tell him no. He was done with pretending that he was fine and dandy as her fuck buddy.

He loved Kate Turner and it was time he told her the truth.

What did he have to lose besides his dignity and his mortal life when she kicked his ass? God, he was a glutton for punishment.

When he sank his key in the lock and opened his door, he was smiling. She might kill him for breaking the rules, but damn, she looked good when she was angry.

[9]

ROCK & KATE

Fresh out of the shower, Kate was considering her options for dinner. Pizza? Tacos? Ah the well-balanced diet of a police officer used to take out rather than making a meal. She stared at the screen for *GrubOnTheGo* and winced when nothing really caught her eye.

It kind of made sense in an odd way. She was only thinking of ordering because she didn't know what else to do with her time. She didn't really own a TV. She streamed shows on her phone or her laptop when the mood struck, but she wasn't in the mood for much of anything.

So, food it was.

She could have sex. But sex meant calling Rock and with a start, she realized that she honestly didn't even know what day it was anymore. Had it just been that morning when she woke up alone in her bed so upset that he'd left without a word?

See? The devil on her shoulder griped at her. *That's what happens when you get attached to someone. Disappointment.*

Kate flopped down onto the bed, staring up at the high

ceiling with its tin ornamental plates, blinking up at the intricate design. *Hey, I thought you're supposed to be the one telling me to call him over?*

I have no problem with you having sexy times. I have a problem with you turning into a sap. That's the angel's department.

The angel was silent. Probably off stuffing her face or having sexy times of her own.

Kate laughed at herself. Angels... yeah, they had to have sex. She'd seen Supernatural. No slouches there in the heaven department. And even Lucifer... damn.

Her laughter only got louder when she realized that yes, she was actually 'talking' to the voices in her head.

"I need to stop before Roan puts me in for a seventy-two-hour hold."

The doorbell rang and she almost launched herself off the bed to get it. Anything was better than having a ridiculous conversation with herself, which could only get her in trouble.

"Coming! Hold on!"

She stopped short of her bedroom door and made a U turn back to her dresser. Digging a pair of shorts out, she pulled those on over her panties, and a t-shirt over her bra. With her luck it was the media descending on her doorstep.

Well, they would just have to deal with an old pair of shorts and a CCPD FAMILY FUN DAY T-shirt.

By the time she made it to the front door she'd given up on trying to tame her hair into a rubber band. She slipped it around her right wrist and opened the door with a smile when she saw who was on her doorstep. "Ronin? What are you doing here?"

The detective shook his head and smiled. "Hello to you too, Kate." He lifted his arm and she saw the plastic bag in his hand with two distinctive containers straining against the thin plastic. "I brought food."

"Oh, bribery of an officer. Good move."

"I know one of your weaknesses."

He started to take a step inside, but she touched a cautionary finger against his chest to keep him in place.

"Hold it right there, mister."

The look he gave her was almost comical.

"You know that's assault, right?"

She dropped her hand back to her side. "Damn, Matsumoto. Are you going to start crying on me? Big bad detective, my ass."

"Inappropriate comments," Ronin nodded thoughtfully. "That's a sexual harassment write up. "You're really piling them on, Kate."

Her smile dropped away. "Well, the more the merrier it seems. Maybe I'll get a group discount for the complaints against me."

Ronin shook his head. "Sorry, I'm not the funny one in the family. Jon Lee would have at least kept his foot out of his mouth for a few more minutes."

That brought a lift back to her smile. "Wow. A whole two minutes! I'd be such a lucky girl." She stepped back from the door and let him step inside. "Seriously. Thanks. I was just trying to figure out what to order in and nothing sounded good."

Setting the bag down on her little table, Ronin looked over at her. "Pizza and tacos didn't cut it?"

Kate rolled her eyes. "Jeez! Do you have surveillance on me?"

His snort was almost a cough. "This area of town only has a few decent places that deliver. I've seen the debris on your desk from when you have stuff delivered at the precinct. It doesn't take a detective to figure it out."

"And yet," she shot back with a mulish expression on her face, "you invaded my squad room to inventory my fast-food trash?"

"Keep this up, Kate," he gestured at the other chair and untied the straps at the top of the bag, "and I'm going to give you chopsticks instead of a fork."

She sat down heavily in the chair and gave him a mutinous look. "It's my kitchen."

They both started to laugh, and Kate sat back with a grin. "Thanks for this."

Ronin looked down at the bowl he held in his hand. "Food?" He handed it to her with a fork on the top of the lid.

"That too." Kate took it from his hands and set it down on the table with a sigh. "But thanks for stopping by. It's nice to see a friendly face at the door. I was half-expecting a deluge of hack reporters looking for a sensationalized interview."

He looked back over his shoulder at the door. "They'll be around. You might want to close all the drapes."

Kate looked up at the bank of windows along the wall and just couldn't muster up the energy to get back up from her chair.

Ronin sat down and opened the top of his bowl and removed the paper from the wooden chopsticks he'd pulled from the bag. "You want me to close the curtains?"

She snorted at the thought as she peeled open the top of her bowl. "If they want pictures of me stuffing my face, go for it. There are worse on the wall in the breakroom at the precinct building."

She knew that Ronin couldn't argue with that.

"Okay, the offer still stands." He lifted his chopsticks from the bowl, somehow managing to hold rice and little bits of veggies between the long wooden sticks.

Kate watched him put the bite in his mouth. "Seriously, that's some kind of magical power you have. If I tried that I'd have the rice all over the front of my t-shirt."

He nodded while he chewed, and when he swallowed he looked up at her. "That's why I brought you a fork."

She shook her head. "You don't want me to look silly?"

He shook his head right back. "Because I don't want you to waste rice. Damn shame to waste good sticky rice like this." When she stared back at him, he shrugged. "Hey, don't look at me like that. My mother would tell you Japanese don't waste rice. It's good healthy food." He lifted his arm and flexed his bicep. *"Make good strong boys."*

She had to fight back the laughter that rose in her throat or choke on the bite of food in her mouth. Hearing Ronin raise his voice up into a higher octave almost sent the rice straight into her nose. Once she forced it down with a few enthusiastic swallows, she got up and pointed toward the kitchen. "You want a drink?"

He nodded. "Looks like I forgot something."

She waved off his self-admonishment. "Beer, water, or soda?"

"Water's great. I have to get back to the station in a bit."

Kate pulled out two cold bottles of water and let the door swing shut. She looked up at the clock on the wall before making her way back to the table, setting a bottle down beside him. "I didn't realize what time it was." She slid back into her chair. "That's the life of someone on suspension, I guess."

It felt like the world was weighing even more on her and she shook it off.

"Don't listen to me." She forced her smile brighter and spoke before he could say something nice to her to excuse her maudlin behavior. "Seriously, Ronin. I don't think I've ever heard you make a joke before." Kate picked up her fork again. "I promise," she waved it over her bowl, "I won't waste any of this."

She took a bite and tried to keep her gaze on the tabletop. But she still saw the look of concern on his face as he watched her. When she got that bite down, she met his gaze again.

"I don't want to have your mother on my back."

The two of them laughed at the idea before Ronin shook his head. "It wouldn't be possible. You two are the same height. She just has about thirty pounds on you."

Kate dropped her chin and stared at him. "You better hope I don't get her phone number and tell her you're discussing her weight." He lost a little color under his normal warm tan. "Just joking, relax. Seriously, though... I guess I don't really get over to your side of the precinct very often."

He set his chopsticks down across the top of his bowl and his eyes focused on her in a way that almost made her sweat.

"Are you about to interrogate me? Cuz, I'll confess." He remained quiet for what seemed like a long, long time. "Seriously, what do you want me to say? You're starting to creep me out."

And unexpectedly, her eyes started to tear up.

Ronin leaned against the table and reached out, putting his hand on her forearm. "I don't want you to confess to anything, Kate. I want you to fight."

She sucked in a breath and her throat almost closed up tight. She fought for her next breath, fighting back the sobs that threatened to overtake what was left of her calm. When she managed to pull that air in, she shook and nodded. "I want to fight. I just don't know how."

Rock felt like the ground under his feet shifted and shook. He'd never experienced a real earthquake, but this had to be worse.

He'd worked himself up on the way over to Kate's apartment. His mind had been struggling to understand what Roan had told him. Kate had been suspended from the CCPD. They'd taken away her badge. And that piece of shit abuser was suing her?

He wanted to tear that asshole limb from limb, but his first thoughts had been to get to Kate.

Rock was sure he could help her somehow. Make her dinner? Rub her feet? Take her out somewhere and let her throw things and scream? Whatever she wanted to do; he'd make it happen.

But then he'd showed up to her apartment and parked behind a strange car.

Someone from work? A friend he didn't know?

And really, that was a wide-open field.

He hardly knew anyone in Kate's life besides her brothers and those he'd only met at odd times when he'd stuck around long after he was supposed to.

He'd even grumbled at himself for not thinking of something to bring to her. Flowers? Something sweet? Hell, even a bottle of whiskey. Something to take away the sting of what was happening.

Rock hadn't counted on... whatever this was.

He recognized the man at the table. He didn't really

know him personally, but in their part of Center City there weren't many Asian officers on the CCPD. Even fewer detectives. And Detective Matsumoto worked with Walker, Kate's brother on a few cases that Station House Twenty-Nine was connected to.

Ronin. That's what people called him. Some kind of reference to something in his heritage. Good for him.

Good for her?

At first, he'd stopped walking thinking that he'd wait for a break in their conversation to knock on the door. And then he'd realized that they were sharing a meal. Conversation. Laughter.

Jealousy wasn't something that Rock wore well. Pain? He was used to that. He'd strained muscles. Broken bones.

But a heart breaking?

That wasn't something he'd felt before.

He'd never cared that much about someone else before.

And now, he guessed that what he'd fooled himself into wanting with Kate, just wasn't in the cards for him.

An incoming text turned his head and Rock backed up until he was well out of sight of the windows.

Something he knew from the time he'd spent at her place. Leaning against the wall, he lifted the phone up and swiped open his text app.

VITALIA: Rock? You okay?

He couldn't help but smile at the message. She had no idea his whole world was falling apart.

> *MF: Fine.*
> *MF: Sorry I left without saying anything. I had to see-*

He stopped short and erased a few characters.

> *MF: Sorry I left without saying anything. I needed some air.*

He sent the text and waited to see if there was a response.

It didn't take long. Vitalia had damn fast fingers.

And a lot more practice with text message than he did.

> *VITALIA: I'm taking Isaac back to his place. Doctor Kaya threatened to hook him up to an IV and sedate him if he didn't spend the night in a real bed. If you need something, call me, okay?*

He shook his head. Aldo Campanelli's daughter wasn't just a firefighter by choice, she'd been a member of the CCFD since birth and her family, a few generations before. She also had a heart of gold and the soul of an angel.

> *MF: You better get some sleep too, young lady. Don't make me call your Mama.*

Gloria Campanelli wouldn't mince words either. She'd tell her daughter just how things were going to be if she thought Vitalia wasn't taking care of herself. Rock had no doubts about that. But he figured the threat would be enough to get his point across.

The next message that popped up was a picture in Vitalia's Jeep. Her baby. Rock could see Isaac asleep in the passenger seat at the edge of the image, but the center was a clear photo of Vitalia sticking out her tongue at him. Childish, but effective.

And damn, he needed something to lighten the mood.

> VITALIA: *Hey, since you've got the rest of the day off. Go and see Kate. I'm sure the two of you can use a distraction. Luv you, Grumpy!*

Well, there went the rest of his heart, crumbling to dust in his chest. Kate already had her distraction. It just wasn't him.

Pushing away from the wall, Rock started back to his truck and stopped again. He looked back at the shallow steps leading up to her door and considered going up there anyway. Like a band-aid. Quick and so damn painful.

Knock. Introduce himself as the outgoing fuck buddy and wish them well.

He didn't even want to think about the chance that Ronin's presence wasn't just about sex. Maybe Kate had finally changed her mind and decided to try a relationship with someone.

And who the fuck was he to think she needed a confrontation anyway?

Being sued and suspended only to have him come over and act like a fucking caveman?

What was he going to do? Beat on his chest like a silverback gorilla? Punch out the guy who was getting what he wanted?

None of the choices seemed right no matter how he looked at it.

What mattered, still mattered.

He'd dropped everything to come and see her because she mattered. She mattered to him.

And even if this was the end of... whatever they had, he didn't have it in him to turn today into a complete cluster fuck.

He might be jealous, hurting, and damn angry, but he didn't have it in him to dump his own heartbreak onto her pain.

She'd never promised him anything. Or rather, she'd promised him nothing. So, he had nothing to complain about.

Hating how easily he'd made the decision to walk away, he did it anyway. Getting into his vintage Ford truck, he drove over to Station Twenty-Nine and parked in the overflow lot. Called a taxi over with a shrill whistle and told the driver, "Ciro's Bar, please."

The driver nodded and lifted his eyes to the rearview mirror. "That the place with the Christmas lights on the ceiling?"

Rock blew out a breath and nodded. "Yeah, that's the place."

"All right. Ciro's it is."

Ronin sat back in his chair and kept his gaze fixed on hers. "Walker said Doc got you an attorney."

Kate sighed and mumbled to herself.

Ronin's smile was a little lop-sided. "It's the benefit and bane of being a first responder in a tight-knit area, Kate. Everyone kind of knows everyone."

"Well," she sighed, "they're my brothers and look

enough like twins that I'm surprised they don't finish each other's sentences."

Ronin shook his head. "If they were twins, I think Walker would have pushed Roan out of the womb. So just be glad they're not. Anyway, the lawyer's good, I looked her up on Caselaw, but what I have in mind is something you might not want to tell her about."

Panic seized her and she tried to shut him down right there.

"No. Nuh-uh. If you're thinking of doing something she wouldn't approve of, no. You're not that kind of officer."

He grinned. "I'm still not that kind of officer, but this isn't something I can actually do. I can set it up and observe, but I don't think I can go to the kinds of places we need to go to make this happen."

Kate leaned back in her chair and put her hand over her heart where her chest was aching. "You're going to give me an anxiety attack talking in circles like this. Just tell me what you have in mind."

He smiled and it was the kind of look like George Peppard's character Hannibal would get on the A-Team. That all knowing, shit-eating grin before he pulled the cigar out of his mouth and drawled, "I love it when a plan comes together."

"This Doug guy, he likes to run his mouth. He put some live video up on Facebook today on the courthouse steps after his lawyer ran his mouth about all kinds of lies." She knew that the unspoken part was 'about you.' "And Dougie? Well, he couldn't keep his mouth shut. Talking about how he was going to take you down. He was going to make you pay for trying to make him look like an ass."

Kate's stomach turned upside down. She swore she

could almost hear him saying those exact words. "Did anyone tell him that he didn't need my help?"

Ronin nodded. "You can tell him that when we get this worked out, okay?"

"And exactly how are we going to get this worked out?" As soon as she asked the question, she was sure she wasn't going to like his answer.

Even though she'd cautioned Ronin just seconds ago about not wanting him to do something questionable, she knew she didn't even have to say that to him. Ronin was one of the good guys, like her brother Walker. He could be a pain in her ass, but he was a damn good police officer. They both made their cases with solid detective work.

"I'm going to head over to Ciro's in a bit and see if I can get a few of the guys from Twenty-Nine to help me with some undercover work."

"Now, hold on-"

"Wow, Walker was right."

That earned him a scathing look.

Ronin held up his hands in surrender. "Hey, don't kill the messenger. Walker said you wouldn't want the guys from Twenty-Nine involved, especially a guy they call... Rock?"

She turned away and stared at the corner.

"So, he was right." Ronin's voice was full of humor. "I'm going to enjoy meeting this man. Seriously though, from what Walker says, which I'm going to have to start listening to him more now, Rock wouldn't be good for this. He'd probably pound Doug into the pavement which wouldn't help your case. Don't worry. No one's going to get physical in this. I just need people who can get close enough to Doug to listen into his conversations. And as private citizens..."

Kate sighed and the ache in her chest eased up. "I trust

you, Ronin. And don't you dare tell my dork of a brother, but I trust Walker too. Please... just let me know how things are going."

Ronin shook his head and dug into the bowl of vegetables and rice in front of him. "As if I'd try to keep you out of the loop." He leaned against the table as he took a bite, managing to speak around it as he looked at her food. "Now, eat."

Kate wrinkled her nose at him. "Yes, Mom."

[10]

ROCK & KATE

Rock sat in the back of the bar at a table by himself. A few of the other guys had seen him and waved him over, but he brushed them off. They knew him well enough to know that they should leave him alone.

And he was enough in his cups that he didn't want to chance losing his temper.

He'd never caused any problems in Ciro's and he wasn't about to start.

Patrick had already given him a cool look and a gentle reminder that he'd be cut off in an instant if he even thought of it. Damn busybody.

The thought had him smiling, at least a little. He had good friends.

Family.

Just not *all* the family he wanted.

"Fuck me."

"Uh, no thanks, Rock. I love you, man, but not like that."

The back door closed softly a few feet away and Rock

looked up. Theo gave him a knowing look. "You okay? Or do you want to talk?"

Rock sat in silence and Theo sighed. "Okay, man. You know I'm here if you need to talk. Or," he looked back over his shoulder toward the door, "if you need someone to take your money at the pool table."

Theo's laughter dimmed a little. "Huh, I wonder what they want."

Rock swung his slightly heavy gaze toward the front of the bar and felt his hackles go up. "Fuck me sideways."

Theo's deep-throated chuckle helped bring him back down. "Again, Rock, not my thing, but hey, you be you."

He walked away toward the bar and Rock sat silently at his table watching as Kate's brother, Walker, got in line behind Theo. And Ronin was standing beside him.

The urge to get up and order another drink at the bar fell away as he reminded himself that he was going to act like a fucking adult.

Sure, he could dream of planting his fist in the other man's face, but that wasn't polite or civilized.

"Fuck polite and civilized."

He snorted at his own gutter humor.

Fuck, he was a little drunk.

Sighing, Rock leaned his head back against the wall and watched the scene unfold in front of him.

The two detectives spoke to Patrick and bought drinks. A couple of beers by the look of it. After they had those in hand, they crossed over to the bank of tables occupied by the firefighters from his house. Walker and... the other guy introduced themselves and sat down to shoot the shit with his friends.

Rock narrowed his eyes at the tables, watching as Pitts shrugged and sat back letting the others talk. Oh, he knew

Pitts was soaking up every word, he wasn't the kind to let a conversation go by without listening in.

It wasn't long before Halo got up to leave. He waved at the crowd and moved to the counter to settle up with Patrick. Greco didn't seem all that involved, but Russell Webb and Reese Rivers were hanging on every damn word. Two of the youngest from Station House Twenty-Nine.

Rock wasn't sure he liked the look of what was going on, but he'd rather roll the hoses on every damn truck in the district than walk over and stick his nose in.

"Shit." Rock let his glass drop down to the tabletop and got up on his feet. The bathroom was down the back hall and he needed to head back there before calling a ride home.

He gave one last look to the group at the table. "Turncoats." With a derisive smile on his face, Rock made his way down the hall to the Men's Room.

His soft groan echoed off the tile as he yanked open the buttons down his fly. It never failed. The time it took to open his fly meant that if he fumbled the buttons at all he might just piss himself before he got his dick out.

He made it, but he grumbled at himself.

Before he met Kate, he'd been a zipper only man, but after he met her... after they'd started their more than satisfying arrangement, she made an offhanded comment about how sexy she thought button fly jeans were and he'd gone out and bought half a dozen.

And let her peel those buttons open to get her hand in his pants.

He should have known back then that he'd never be able to keep up the arrangement. He was a sucker.

For Kate.

The door opened up and Rock gave himself a good strong shake before setting himself to rights.

The stall doors didn't open or close.

And no one stepped up beside him at the urinals.

That left only one possibility.

Rock looked up into the mirror above the sinks and glared at Ronin Matsumoto. "You got a good look?"

Ronin raised a brow but didn't speak.

Shrugging, Rock crossed to the double sink and started washing his hands. "Did you forget why you came in here?"

When Ronin didn't answer right away, he dropped his gaze down to his hands and concentrated on the hot water working through the bubbles. When he shut off the water and reached for a paper towel, he heard Ronin speak for the first time.

"Are you just naturally this much of an ass?"

Flinging the paper towel into the trash, Rock turned around and leaned on the counter. "You just naturally a stalker?"

It wasn't that Ronin smiled. It was that he smiled like he knew something and Rock, well he just wasn't sober enough to hold his tongue.

"Is there a reason you came in here tonight? Don't cops have their own bars to piss in?"

The detective laughed.

Not just a chuckle or a 'ha ha.' No, Detective Matsumoto laughed hard enough to narrow his eyes as his shoulders shook.

"Walker said they call you Rock. I didn't realize it was because you were dense."

Dense?

Dense!

Rock folded his arms across his chest and stared back. "I saw you at Kate's today."

That shook him up. Ronin tilted his head and stared back at Rock. "You saw me there, but you... didn't knock?" He lifted his chin and shook his head. "Is there something I should know?"

Oh, the sheer magnitude of things this asshole didn't know.

"This is a tough time for her." Rock wanted to make sure Ronin knew the score. "And don't think I'm going to give you a pass just because you carry a badge."

The man had the nerve to look like he didn't understand.

"Just be good to her, man. She deserves it."

Rock couldn't think of what else to say. And the alcohol he'd downed when he arrived at Ciro's was starting to hit him... hard.

He decided to leave before he made himself look like a total lightweight and lost the ability to walk out with his head held high.

Fake it, at least in front of the other man. Try to hold on to at least a shred of his dignity.

The hallway was empty when Rock stepped out and he breathed a sigh of relief. All he had to do was walk out of the bar and call himself a damn taxi. Simple.

He didn't make it more than two steps before a hand clamped down on his shoulder. "Wait-"

Rock spun and the world continued to spin with complete disregard to his equilibrium.

The punch that he'd intended to land only threw him off balance and he found himself pushed up against the wall.

To add insult to injury, Walker sidled up and gave him a knowing look. "You're drunk, man."

"Then leave me alone." He growled the words as he tried to shrug Ronin's restraining forearm that was pushed into his chest. "I'm going home."

He'd missed something.

Somewhere.

There was an odd look that passed between the two detectives. He wanted to get mad at them, but at the moment, he just wanted to be alone. And alone meant getting them off his back one way or another.

"If you're going to kick my ass, go ahead and do it. Only you might want to take this out into the parking lot."

That same looked passed between them again and Rock was done. He put all of his frustration into one move, pushing off the wall and away from them.

They didn't try to stop him, and he was glad. He had no interest in hurting anyone else. He just needed to be alone.

He was going to be alone for the foreseeable future anyway, he might as well get used to it.

By the time the taxi dropped his ass off at home, he felt like every single footfall in the stairwell was exploding in his skull. The shockwaves of sound were deafening.

It only took three tries to unlock the door and he was fairly sure he managed to lock it behind him. Then again, there were only two other apartments on his floor that were occupied. A pair of elderly sisters had apartments side by side.

They weren't going to cause any trouble.

Rock threw his phone down on the bed and pulled off his shirt. That was a challenging affair on its own. If he'd remembered that he was wearing a button-down he might not have tried to reach up and pull it off like a t-shirt.

He could replace buttons, but the tear in the back? Not so much.

His jeans and boxers went next, leaving him bare in the chill of his apartment.

Rock's thoughts drifted to Kate as they often did, and the reaction was instantaneous. He was hard and hungry. In his head, she was sitting across from him at a restaurant. Her eyes dark and hungry like his.

The strap of her dress was about to slip down off her shoulder and her lips... fuck, her lips... they were parted, and he could see a little glimpse of the tongue she'd used so well to lick him clean after she'd blown his mind.

Picking his phone up off the bed he considered calling her and then shoved that thought aside. He didn't know exactly how late it was, but he didn't think she'd want a call from him.

Hell, she might not even be alone.

A message. He could send her a text.

That sounded like a horrible idea, but it didn't stop him from signing into his app and that's when he saw it.

Sitting there in his text app.

> MF: *Have to go to med Seth worse not sure if you were fine with me staying this long talk to you later*

Just sitting there, still in the little bubble area just above the keyboard.

Had he really been in so much of a rush that he hadn't even hit the SEND on his text?

As if the day couldn't get any worse than that.

He was mad.

At himself.

One careless moment and he'd left her hanging. He hadn't even called to check on her.

He hit SEND.

Might as well.

Then Rock typed out an explanation.

> *MF: I feel like an ass, Katie*
> *MF: should've checked to make sure it sent, but I was in a rush*
> *MF: no excuse though*
> *MF: Just wanted you to know*
> *MF: Saw Roan at MED heard what happened*
> *MF: you've got to be hurting*
> *MF: I'm here for you*
> *MF: whatever you need*
> *MF: anything*

He lay there staring at the screen. He saw his whole line of messages and looked down at the bottom, wondering if she'd even gotten the messages. Maybe she was asleep.

> *MF: hope you're getting some sleep*
> *MF: when you're awake, call me and let me know how you are*
> *MF: Kate,*

Rock paused staring at the screen and the single word he'd typed out. He knew what he wanted to say, but he had a feeling it would be a huge mistake.

Then again, he wondered, *at least my batting average can't get any worse.*

> MF: *Kate, you need to know that I love you.*
> MF: *I don't just want you some nights.*
> MF: *I don't just want the sex.*
> MF: *I want you to know that this isn't going to go away on my end.*
> MF: *And yes, I should have said this to you*
> MF: *in person*
> MF: *but I just can't help but feel like I've already lost you before we ever started. That's why I needed to say this.*
> MF: *Let's talk. I go back on shift tomorrow so, the day after? Just let me know.*
> MF: *Go ahead and yell at me then if you feel like, but I'd rather just talk so I can plead my case for more with you.*

Leaving his phone on, Rock laid it beside him and closed his eyes. The exhaustion. The frustration. And yes, the alcohol already had his eyelids heavy and his body aching for sleep. It wasn't long before he was completely out.

K ate woke up the next morning and picked up her phone.

An early morning message from her lawyer. She had the paperwork for the actual court case and Kate texted her back with her available time for a meeting.

Which was anytime. It's not like she had to go to work.

She'd already avoided an early visit from Pilar.

As much as she cared for her people and yes, Pilar was going to be her sister-in-law, there were still things she needed to do. And sometimes that was reinforcing that wall that she kept towering above her.

There were huge cracks in the foundation and chunks had fallen out and into disrepair.

That was all her fault.

Becoming Pilar's friend outside of work had made a few holes, adding new friendships through Rock, and going to Ciro's. Those had weakened the wall too.

Rock.

She shook her head.

The day before, after Ronin left, she'd cleaned up. Looking for a new trash bag to put into the wastebasket, she'd found a bottle of her favorite wine.

She didn't own a corkscrew, but this bottle didn't need one. Vitalia Campanelli had brought one to her as a housewarming gift and it had certainly warmed Kate's insides. Sweet and easy it was a wine that she liked a lot.

So much so that Kate had drained the entire bottle last night over a few hours of time and that had been all she needed to put her mess out of her mind.

And yet, while the wine had masked her worry about the lawsuit, it only reminded her about the one person she couldn't push out of her head.

Rock.

Martin.

Martin Ferris.

She smiled. Ferris. Rock. Yeah, she'd been drunk enough the night before to have a good long laugh over the naming game that someone had obviously played in giving Rock his distinctive nickname.

HER ROCK

Kate wondered if they also knew that Rock had one hell of a cock. Long, thick, and curved up toward his belly.

Just thinking about it had her aching. Made her legs squeeze together to ease some of the need she felt.

No.

Kate straightened up and shook her head. She wasn't going to mope about this. About him. She had enough to worry about.

Leaving her phone on the bed she darted into the bathroom to splash some cold water on her face. That should wake her up from La La Land and bring her back to the Island of People who live in Reality!

She might have scrubbed at her face a little too hard, but it didn't really matter. Kate wasn't trying to impress anyone after all.

PING

Her phone's alert caught her attention.

That oddly mechanical ping told her that she had an unread message in her texts.

Snatching a hand towel up from her drawer, Kate gave her face a quick pat-down and went after her phone. If she was lucky it was Serena texting her back with a meeting time.

If her luck sucked, it would be another cryptic message from Walker.

Ever since the meeting with Ronin, her brother had apparently latched onto the concept of the slight subterfuge they were going to use in hoping to discredit Doug Fitchett. She'd received a bunch of messages from him all night long. Every single one was just a random phrase that sounded like it came out of a Cold War Era Spy Thriller.

BestBro: the eagle is nesting in the oak tree

Seeing his 'name' on there always made her grimace. It was the first and only time she'd left her phone in a room with Walker. Sure, she could have changed it back, but it was a nice reminder of what a sneaky jerk Walker could be.

> *BestBro: the tulips are not what they seem*
> *BestBro: tater tots!*

Okay, well, maybe that one was just an observation, but there were more than a dozen of the phrases, sent one at a time and in that odd, stilted language.

Life, her life at least, was just one random moment at a time, punctuated by crazy.

Lifting the phone in her hand she opened the text app and stopped short.

The only thread with bolded text was from MF – Martin Ferris.

Rock.

Damn it.

Her heart stuttered in her chest and then burst to life at the thought of a message. Teenage girl-ish? Maybe, but then again, she'd never really had a boyfriend at that age.

Boyfriend.

She shook the thought away and opened the app.

First glance told her she had a whole slew of messages from him. It was crazy how excited she was to see them.

As she read through Rock's messages she sat down on the edge of her bed and struggled to breathe.

No.

No.

This was not what she wanted!

Love?

Love her?

No. Not like this.

Her chest rose and fell in strange stuttering gasps.

This was why she'd set rules! There was a way to do this where they didn't get hurt.

And Rock had blown that all up!

He said he was in love with her.

Her belly ached, her skin felt clammy, and the heart in her chest pounded out a frantic rhythm.

"No," she shook her head, "this isn't what I wanted."

Kate lay back on the bed and closed her eyes.

There he was.

There was something so raw about Rock. He was strength. He was a good man. His friends had his back and loved him like family. She didn't want that from him.

She wanted his hungry kisses, his talented hands, and yes, his big hard cock.

And she had that over and over again. She'd had him and let him walk away.

His words.

That whole long line of messages sent to her just after midnight had done what nothing else could have.

It pulled her wall down.

Being with him could be a huge mistake. He might fall out of love with her.

Or he might decide that she just wasn't worth the work.

It was all possible, but maybe, so was being happy?

Turning her head toward the clock on the wall she could see that it was too late to talk to him before his shift.

And yes, he'd be available again in just under a day, but she didn't want to wait to talk to him.

Getting back onto her feet, Kate headed straight for the bathroom before she remembered that she'd already brushed her teeth and washed her face.

Clothes!

She needed to wear more than her t-shirt and the boy-shorts panties she had on.

Sweater and jeans. Socks and sneakers.

She grabbed up her phone and her keys.

Kate ignored the mirror on the wall. It was better she didn't see what a mess she was. If she stopped to put on makeup, he'd never recognize her, and if he loved her, makeup wouldn't matter.

She'd worry about the girl thing later.

For now, she needed to find the man.

[11]

ROCK & KATE

Four calls in a row had the entire shift on edge. A Carbon Monoxide alarm, a 911 call for a possible heart attack, a fire in a dorm room where a college student was trying to impress a girl by making a meal in a toaster oven using a coffee pot, and the current call that they were speeding to was an upscale senior retirement community.

Rock leaned forward in his seat as the radio crackled and blared bits and pieces of information, giving them a window into the current situation.

- One engine on scene
- Alarms going off all over the structure
- Three stories of apartments
- Reports of residents trapped in an elevator
- Reports of residents trapped in apartments

Basic chaos with a side of WTF thrown in. Before they arrived at the structure, Faust was already giving them their marching orders.

"Chief is sending us around to the back of the structure.

A report came in from a neighboring building that at least two people are trapped in their apartments on that side. Stairway is clear." He met Rock's eyes with his own and Rock nodded.

"We'll clear it as we go."

Faust nodded and spared a glance for the rest of Rescue Crew. "Be fast, be careful, remember what's at stake."

The mood inside the Rescue Truck was thick with warning. They all knew what Faust was talking about. Seth might be out of the woods, but nothing was a guarantee. Nothing.

Rock knew that more than most. He might be the oldest on crew, but he was also the man with the most years in the CCFD. Turning to look at Lofton sitting beside him, Rock clamped a hand down on his shoulder. "You heard the LT, right?"

It took Lofton a moment to react and Rock grabbed a hold of his turnout gear and gave him a shake.

"Yeah, yeah..." Lofton gave him a hard look and tried to shake him off.

Rock didn't let go. "I'm serious, Lofton. Joking at the house is one thing, on a call like this we focus, or we don't come back." Even with the sirens running, the inside of the truck was eerily quiet. "We're all going to have our hands busy. If you fuck up, chances are you're going to take one of us with you."

The anger in Lofton's eyes died out and he nodded weakly. His voice wasn't much better. "Yeah. Yeah, Rock. I get it."

"Okay!" Faust leaned forward and looked at the street. "Let's pull up over there, Reese. We'll be out of the way enough for other vehicles, but we'll have easy access to the stairwell."

The next few minutes rolled on like a silent movie to Rock. Everyone jumped out of the Rescue Truck, grabbed their gear, and made their way to the stairwell closest to the apartments where victims had been seen waving in the windows.

Looking up at the sky above the complex, Rock saw two wispy trails of gray smoke rising up into the air. From what he could tell, they weren't all that close.

Faust stopped beside him and followed his gaze. "Never a good sight."

Rock nodded and blew out a breath. "We have our jobs to do." He held up a closed fist and Faust bumped his own against it.

"Let's go!"

The crew members jogged to the stairwell entrance and began their climb.

Kate knew she looked like crap, but Rock had seen her sweaty and naked enough times that he wouldn't care, right? Pulling into the parking lot at Station Twenty-Nine, she saw the empty apparatus floor and cursed under her breath.

She pushed open her door and let it slam shut behind her. It didn't take long to find the Administration Office.

At Kate's knock, she heard a soft voice. "Come in!"

The inner office was fairly sparse as far as furniture went. A desk, a couple of chairs and a bookshelf full of boxes and binders. The woman sitting behind the desk, gestured her forward. "Hey there! How can I help you today?"

"I wanted to stop by and see one of the firefighters, but

all the vehicles are gone." Kate's gaze dropped down to the brass nameplate on the desk between two thriving plants. 'FINOLA CARISSI' was printed in perfect capital letters and under it, the words 'Administrative Assistant' were visible. Someone had added a sticky note at the edge with big, bold handwritten letters spelling out '& GODDESS' with a jaunty exclamation point at the end.

Finola's easy smile faltered a little. "They've been out for a few hours already. It's almost a record-breaking pace today," she divulged. "The last call I heard about was a suspected fire at an assisted living facility between Houston Blvd and-"

"Hughes?" Kate felt her brow furrow. "Ashland Assisted Living?"

"Yes! How do you know?"

Kate shrugged. "I work for CCPD. I'm-"

"Rock's friend." Finola pushed back her chair and stood, offering a hand. "I don't think I've ever seen you here."

Kate tried to let that question roll on by. "You said suspected fire?"

Finola leaned down and looked into her computer screen. "It's a strange one. At least half a dozen fire alarms all over the building. I think they've got three companies down there. It's a lot of stuff to check."

"Especially with seniors who might need assistance to evacuate." Kate was already walking before she remembered her manners. "Thanks! Ah... nice to meet you-"

"Finola! You too, Sergeant Turner! Take care!"

It should have bothered her that Aldo's assistant knew about her. Rock's friend. She'd said those words, but the look in her eyes said more.

Either Finola was extremely observant, or Kate wasn't at all.

Who else knew about Rock's feelings before she did?

Kate brushed off the feelings that crept up on her.

This wasn't the time to start asking questions like that. She had to talk to Rock first.

By the time she got back to her car she felt another sensation that took precedence over her curiosity. Worry.

As an officer, she'd been called to her share of fires. The kind of event that Finola was describing was one that had its own share of dangers. Elderly. Multiple floors.

Picking up her phone she did a quick search for news.

Almost a dozen links popped up.

Street video from bystanders.

Local news stations on the scene.

Nothing gave her a clear view of trucks in the vicinity. And while she could see a number of firefighters in view of the cameras, she couldn't see the names on the back of their bunker gear.

Switching apps, she made a call.

The phone rang just twice before it was picked up.

"Kate! Oh hey! Uh... I'm at work."

Kate could hear the hesitant tone in Irish's voice. "Sorry, I know. That's why I'm calling."

"Oh!" Irish perked up. "I might be called away, but until then I'm all yours. What's up?"

"The fire at Ashford? What can you tell me?"

"Hmm... One sec, okay?"

"Yeah, sure." Kate leaned back against her car seat and tried to focus on something innocuous. It didn't work. An odd feeling in her gut made her suck in a breath and let it out slowly. "One sec."

"Kate?"

"Yes!" Kate almost stepped on Irish's question. "What is it?"

"If you're looking for the firefighters from Twenty-Nine, they're all there. The two ambo crews. Truck, engine, and rescue. I can see them on the CCTV feed on one of my screens."

Kate swallowed and blew out a breath. "Can you tell anything about what's going on? Is the building on fire or are they still looking for the source of the alarms?"

"Let me see..." She could hear Irish murmuring to herself. "I'm trying to listen into the radio calls coming through the shared system. I can see two... two sources of smoke coming from different structures on the roof. I think they're coming out of vents of some sort. It's hard to see through the smoke itself.

"Hmm. I... I think... yes. The truck was sent around to the west side of the building to get their ladder up and help with some evacuations. Goodness, that's going to be kind of scary, especially from the third floor! And I can see both Ambos on the street, inside the barrier. Gordon's Ambo is closer to Thirtieth Street. Whoa!"

"Irish?" Kate's eyes closed tight. "What?"

"Uh... Kate? There's smoke pouring out of the far side of the structure. Let me try and find another camera view."

Kate put her phone on speaker and punched up the volume and set it down on the console between the seats of her car. Turning over the engine with a heavy twist of her key, she put her car in reverse and looked back over her shoulder as she backed up.

She could hear Irish talking through everything she was finding.

Until she stopped short.

"Center City Nine-One-One. What is your emergency?"

A call must have come into the dispatch office. Kate

hung up and continued to drive. She knew, probably better than most, the fastest way to get to Ashland Assisted Living Center. When it first opened a few years before, Kate had been the supervisor on a case that started there. Her officers had collected information and it had been turned over to the detectives who would finish the investigation, but she knew her way around the center. At least enough that she could find the Rescue Crew.

It was insanity. Really. Going down to a major rescue attempt? A fire?

She wasn't an officer at the moment. She was just a civilian, racing to an emergency... why?

Rock's words replayed in her head.

Leave it to him to dump all of these feelings on her and then when she finally gets his messages, he's what? Pulling people out of a building on fire?

A light up ahead seemed to turn red at the drop of a hat. Kate stopped behind the line and leaned forward looking up into the sky.

She could see smoke against the clouds, and it wasn't just two whisps like she'd read about online. These were columns of smoke, thick and dark.

A horn behind her blared and she flinched. Putting her focus on the road ahead, she eased her car forward and back on track toward the fire.

Somewhere to the left of her, a car was pumping out the bass and she wanted to glare at them. She had enough on her mind.

Rock.

Damn it.

No, she wasn't really blaming him for the messages he'd sent.

It wasn't about blame.

It was like she'd missed the whole thing to begin with. Like she hadn't been a necessary part of this... this what?

She shuddered at the emotions that her thoughts were bringing up. Emotions she didn't have a name for and really didn't want to examine all that closely. This was exactly why she didn't do relationships.

They made her crazy!

Another red light! She slammed both of her palms against the steering wheel and a siren cut through the heavy blanket of her thoughts.

Up ahead a firetruck went through an intersection and Kate felt her heartbeat pick up its speed, almost double of what it had been a few moments before.

As she waited for the light to change back to green, she grumbled under her breath. "You better fucking be okay." Her shoulders sagged. "Jerk."

Rock was struggling to move through the hallway. The smoke was closing in on them. They still had a few more people to evacuate from the building, but the way things were going, the way the smoke was starting to pour into the hallway, it was becoming a real possibility that the Chief was going to pull them out before they could reach the last two.

Greco and Reese were already headed back down with their last evacuee. An elderly man with both legs amputated, he hadn't stood a chance to get down the stairs. They'd almost had to pry him out of his bed when they'd reached him. He'd already accepted the fact that he was going to die.

Hopelessness.

Rock had seen the look in the older man's eyes. And even when they swore they could get him out, he clung to his sheets with a death grip. It had been Reese that broke through to him enough that he'd allowed them to help instead of fight against them.

The youngest of the Rescue Crew, Reese, was becoming a huge asset to the group.

A voice broke through the dull roar inside his mask.

"Rock? Are you close?"

Trying to project more confidence than he had into his voice, Rock answer back. "Chief, I think we're almost there."

"Visibility."

"It sucks."

He could see Aldo's withering look in his mind.

"Sorry, Chief. It's thick up here. Getting darker by the minute."

"Mmmhmm." Rock knew how much the Chief agonized over every order. "You said you're close?"

Rock knew by the schematic of the building that they were maybe three rooms from the two elderly women trapped in their shared suite. "Yeah, Chief. I think we can make it." He blew out a breath as he gave his head a shake. "As long as the level of smoke holds."

The radio crackled for a moment before Aldo Campanelli's warm and comforting voice reached his ears. "If that smoke starts getting darker by the second, get out of there. You hear me, Rock?"

"I hear you, sir. I hear you." He ground his back teeth together. "See you in a few."

Another step and Rock felt a hand tug at his arm.

He didn't stop and barely threw a look over his shoulder, choosing to shout instead of trying to use the radio. "What?"

Lofton's mask was nearly covered in fog on the inside. "I can't do this, man. I can't."

"I need you, Lofton. There are two ladies in there who need you."

The younger firefighter shook and the emergency lighting that reflected off the front of his mask made him look inhuman. "The walls, Rock. The walls are closing in on me."

Shit. The guy was having a total breakdown in the middle of a rescue.

It was no use yelling at him. What would that accomplish? It wouldn't get him to the women, and they needed his help.

"Okay." He called in on his radio. "Chief? Lofton needs to turn back. Can you send someone into the stairwell to meet him? Help him back out?"

He could hear the weary tone in the Chief's voice. "Faust, you got this?"

The audio that came out of the open line almost made Rock deaf for a moment, the residual sound blaring in his ears.

As Faust called for another crew member to go with him, Rock gave Lofton a nudge with his shoulder. "Go before you fall down. I won't have the strength to carry you out too."

Rock turned back down the hall and started walking again. He'd lost precious time mitigating the panic attack that Lofton was struggling with.

He didn't really blame the guy. They were all afraid, sometimes more than others. It wasn't really about blame or speed, it was about being dependable. And Rock couldn't stop to help Lofton. He just had to push him in the right direction so he could attend to their assignment.

They were two women short of clearing the whole top floor of this wing of the Ashland building. And he was going to find a way to make it happen.

He just hoped he hadn't lost count.

Coming to a stop at what looked like the last door of the hall, Rock closed his hand into a fist and pounded on the door. "Fire Department! Call out if you can hear me!"

Nothing.

He repeated the call and then leaned into the door to listen.

Nothing!

Rock lifted his hand again stopping when he heard the small keening cry of someone in pain.

"Shit." He raised his voice, trying to direct his voice into the dark to find her. "I'm coming in, stand away from the door!"

Rock took a step back and then another. After that, one second was all he needed to break the door in, almost off its hinges. Pieces of wood flung into the interior of the room.

"Fire Department! Call out!"

It wasn't the answer he was looking for, but Rock could hear a woman sobbing across the room.

He moved as quickly as he could, moving anything that could be in the way of their path getting out, using the head of his Halligan tool. The sounds came from the corner by the window and when he managed to come up beside the bed his heart nearly broke into pieces.

One woman lay still in the bed, her eyes open and unseeing and her jaw slack. Kneeling beside her, was the other occupant of the suite, her sister. Pulling off his glove, Rock reached over and felt for a pulse. He could tell at a glance that it wasn't necessary, but it was policy and really it could help her sister to understand.

"Ma'am." He touched her shoulder, and she shook him off. "Ma'am, we have to go."

"No," her voice was slightly muffled, but he could hear enough of her clipped syllables to understand, "I'm not leaving. My sister-"

"I can't take you both, ma'am. Your sister, she's gone."

"I will be to, if you let me stay."

He heard that tone in her voice, the horrible ache of grief.

He understood her feelings, but he couldn't just leave her to die. "Ma'am please." Rock bent over lifted her up from the floor.

At first, he couldn't tell if she was actively fighting him because of the bulk of his bunker-gear, but as he pulled her to her full height, he realized exactly what she was doing.

She'd gone limp, almost sliding through his hold.

Going down on one knee, Rock removed his helmet and then his mask, turning it to cover her face so she could have some clean air to breathe. "Ma'am. I'm so sorry for your loss, but I can't leave you here like this. I can't. Please, for our safety, I'm going to ask you not to fight me on this."

She tilted her chin up, she glared at him through his mask. "Leave me alone. I don't want to leave her."

The look in her eyes almost killed him with the intensity of her grief. He couldn't quite remember where, but he'd seen that look before. Mindless grief and desperation. He shook off the thought and blew out a breath. "I'm sorry, but I'm not going to leave you either. Take a deep breath, ma'am. We're about to walk through hell together."

She may have hated him in that moment, but the

woman beside him took in a deep, lung expanding breath before she nodded.

Rock slipped his mask back over his face, took a good look at his oxygen level and then grabbed up his helmet. He was going to get this woman to safety and deal with the rest of it later. He was damn good at that.

He swept her up and set her over his shoulder as gently as he could. She was already frail, her bones fragile and easily broken. There was no sense in doing damage to her trying to save her life, so with a deep breath and a prayer, Rock headed back down the hallway toward the stairs.

"Kate!"

She heard her name, but she didn't turn to look at who was saying it. The voice sounded vaguely familiar, but the one thing she knew was that it wasn't Rock.

"Kate! Over here!"

She heard the heavy footfalls of boots, but she couldn't tear her eyes off of the building. The top floor was nearly full engulfed in flames and she'd already scanned the ground outside the building for Rock. And she hadn't found him.

"Hey, what are you doing here?"

She felt a familiar weight on her shoulder and looked up into the eyes of Lieutenant Gibson Braun, her friend and landlord. "Are... are your people okay?"

He nodded and cast a look at the building before looking back at her. "Are you looking for Rock?"

Great. Talk about being transparent, hmm?

"Yeah, I stopped by the house and heard that y'all were here. Is Rescue on another side of the building?"

He shook his head and gestured toward the door near the corner of the structure. "Rescue's almost out."

"Almost?" She looked at the group of firefighters waiting at the corner. "Who's missing?"

She counted the people hovering by the door. "He's still in there, isn't he?"

Gibson set his arm around her shoulders. "They have one more resident to extract. Then once we're sure no survivors are left in the building; we'll knock that fire down."

"But Rock-"

"He'll be out in a minute, just watch."

Gibson gave her shoulders a squeeze. "I've got to go. Are you going to be okay here?"

The truth? She didn't think he wanted the truth, but he was busy enough that she gave him the right answer. "Go... be amazing."

He jogged off, calling out orders to his men as Kate fought the urge to move closer. If she had her uniform on it wouldn't have been a problem. Police usually worked a scene like this, keeping the civilians and looky-loos away.

Now she could be tossed out behind the barricades and she'd have no reason to complain. The door to the stairwell remained closed and Kate saw the growing agitation of the other members of crew, Faust specifically.

She knew the hell they'd gone through with Seth recently. Word like that moved swiftly through the community of first responders, bad and good.

When Faust started to move, so did she. Standing back just wasn't going to cut it anymore.

If someone was going to drag that infuriating man out of a burning building, it was going to be her, just so she could get grumpy and pissed about him breaking the rules.

She saw the shocked expression of a CCPD officer as she ran past him, but he didn't even try to stop her. At least her notoriety was good for something, like being recognized outside of her uniform.

No one tried to stop her, at least until she reached the group of firefighters from Twenty-Nine, but the man who got a hand on her arm dropped it as the stairwell door opened up and Kate could finally breathe again.

[12]

ROCK & KATE

Rock didn't make it more than a few steps outside of the door before he was surrounded. Two other crew members helped to lift the older woman from his shoulder and as he watched, EMTs Ramsey and Raffe brought a gurney over. Moments later, the elderly woman had been given a quick exam and wheeled off toward Ambo Nineteen.

Greco appeared beside him with a wet cloth and Rock pulled off his mask and scrubbed at the soot and stains he'd gotten on his skin when he'd given his mask to the victim before he'd brought her out of the building.

Greco's hand was heavy on his shoulder. "You took your damn time coming out."

Rock turned his head toward his friend and swallowed down the lump in his throat. "I had to get her to leave her sister." He saw the wide-eyed look on his friend's face. "She was already gone when I got there. Her sister wanted to stay." Saying the words out loud only made the pang of grief worse. "She wanted to die there with her."

"You did the right thing, man."

Nodding, Rock took another pass at his face, cooling off his skin after the heat inside the building. "I'm not sure she's going to agree with it." His gaze strayed over to the Ambo sitting near the barricades that CCPD had put up to mark the edge of the active scene. While the two EMTS prepared to lift the gurney into the back of the Ambo, he could see the racking sobs that shook her shoulders, her face hidden in her free hand. "I don't think she wanted to survive without her sister."

"Maybe," Greco's voice was softer than normal, "but you don't get to make that kind of decision for her. Even if that's what she told you, your job... our job, is to bring people out. To save those who can be saved."

"I know. I just hope she's going to be okay." He turned to his friend. "What's next?"

Greco pointed toward the base of one of the ladder trucks parked along Hughes Drive. Chief Campanelli was standing with Faust and Gibson and a couple of other officers. "As soon as you were clear, they opened up the hoses on the ladder trucks. They're trying to knock down the fire. And the crew on Engine Forty-Seven is on another corner putting out some fires at street level. You should go and have Harmony or Vega check you out for inhalation."

Rock waved off the idea. "I'm okay. I just-"

"And I think someone's here to see you."

Rock slanted a look at Greco. "What the hell are you talking about?"

Stretching out his arm, Greco pointed toward the edge of the scene near one of the barricades. "Over there."

He followed his friend's outstretched hand.

"Kate."

She lifted her hand in a hesitant wave and he couldn't help but drink in the sight of her standing there. It was like that first breath of oxygen after walking through a smoke-filled hallway. He felt alive.

Greco gave him a shove. "Go, see what's up. We probably won't have anything to do until overhaul."

Nodding, Rock touched his radio where it was clipped to his coat. "I have my radio."

Chuckling, Greco gave him a wink. "Now, go get your girl."

He wanted to jog over to where she was, but he needed the time it would take to walk. He needed to pull himself together. Time to try and guess what she was thinking.

He drew a blank. Kate's expression was guarded, and he had no idea what that meant. Still, he wanted to be near her. Wanted to get close enough to feel her warmth.

He wasn't sure what to expect at all. Not from Kate. She liked to keep him guessing.

When he was close enough to touch her, he stopped, his eyes moving over her face, hungry for the sight of her.

"Kate? Are you okay?"

Her head shook. "Me? Am I okay?" Kate's hand gestured toward Ashland. "You just walked out of a burning building with a woman over your shoulder. You've got soot... smoke... whatever all over you, and you ask me if I'm okay?"

"Yeah," he nodded and leaned closer, "I'm worried about you, Katie."

The tears that sprang into her eyes worried him. He watched as she blinked them back furiously. "I'm fine. I really am."

"I want to believe you, but I can see it in your eyes." He

licked at his dry lips and saw her eyes follow the movement. "Did I do that, Katie? Is it my fault?"

He could almost see her tremble before him, and Rock wasn't so sure if the thought scared him or made him hot. Either way, it didn't matter as long as she wanted him around.

"If I did, I hope you're going to give me a chance to apologize. Make it up to you. Somehow." He was short of breath around her. His lungs pulling in a lot of air when he was standing still. "I guess you got my messages."

Kate nodded, such a slight movement but he caught it. "I read them, and I don't know what to think. I don't know what to feel."

"You don't have to think anything." He wanted to reach out and touch her arm, comfort her, but Kate was always hesitant about touching like that. Comfort wasn't exactly something she accepted from others. He'd seen her give it, but receiving it was something she seemed to find uncomfortable. "You can feel whatever you want. I messed up the other day. My text didn't send, but I should have called you to make sure you knew why I left."

"You don't have to do any of that." Her lips pressed into a thin white line for a moment. "We're adults. We're not in a relationship, we-"

"I want to change that."

Fuck. He'd just cut her off mid-sentence.

"Sorry, I didn't mean to interrupt-"

"But you did." She smiled... a little. "And so, did I. Again, we're adults we can do that too. We can also acknowledge that it's probably rude." She blew out a breath. "I went to Twenty-Nine looking for you. Came here when I heard about the fire. Seeing you come out of that building was a relief. I honestly don't know exactly how I feel about what you said to me in your messages. I want to say I do, but I think it's jumbled me up inside even more than I was before I read them."

"Okay." He felt like she'd just reached into his chest and wrapped her hand around his heart. Painful? Yes. But at least she hadn't told him to fuck off and leave her alone. It was much better than that. "I have to go back in when the fire's out."

Kate nodded and gave him a weak smile. "Overhaul, I think they... you call it."

He nodded. "We make sure that there aren't any hotspots left or embers that can flare up after we're gone."

"Walker would say you're just destroying evidence if this was an arson."

He hesitated. "I don't know what they're going to find when OFI goes in there. It's their job to investigate fires. We just make sure they go out and stay that way."

Rock saw her look toward the building and followed her gaze. The smoke that was still churning out of the top floor had her attention.

"You were in there."

It wasn't a question, but he heard uncertainty in her voice.

"And I came out alive. In one piece."

"And a fucking hero."

Her cheeks pinked a little and Rock fought off the urge to lean into her.

"When I get off tomorrow morning, you want me to come over?"

He hadn't meant the hint of a double entendre, but there wasn't time for finesse.

"I was wondering," he saw that hesitation again, "if I

could go over to your place. I checked the doorbell cam at my place, and I've got a few reporters waiting for me."

Just the thought of her in his space made him hard. Wearing as much gear as he was, he didn't have to worry about someone seeing it. "My keys are in my locker back at the station, but I can call the property office in the building and they'll give you a spare."

He rattled off the address and watched as she backed away.

"I'll see you later, Rock."

"I can't wait, Katie."

There was a slight smile on her lips, and he was going to hold onto that image for a long time. A little over twenty hours of time.

Parking in his assigned stall under his building, Rock looked down at the screen on his phone.

> *MF: you wake up okay?*
> *KATE: overslept*

He grinned and picked up his phone and sent another message.

> *MF: I picked up breakfast*
> *MF: probably should have asked first*
> *KATE: shut up! You brought food!*
> *MF: and coffee*
> *KATE: I ducking love you*

Rock sat there looking at the screen wondering if there would be another message.

Then, he decided to get out of the car. The food was going to get cold and he wanted to see her. They could discuss the rest later.

MF: Relax, Katie
MF: I'm headed up

P acing.
Pacing was good.
Pacing helped to get out some of her nerves.
And her frustrations.
And her worries.
"Shit."

She could run a marathon right at that very moment and it wouldn't do a thing to calm her down.

What the hell was she thinking?

She'd typed out – I fucking love you.

And sent it before she could think better of it.

The only thing that saved her impulsive move was auto-correct changing it into DUCKING.

She blew out a breath and wondered if there was still time to escape before he got up to the apartment.

She heard the distinctive scratch of a key pushing into the lock on the front door.

Nope. Too late.

Rock opened the door slowly, looking toward the wall.

"I left the chain off."

With a soft chuckle, he pushed the door open and stood there in the frame of the door.

She had lost her mind, because inside of her head, she was imagining what it would be like if he called out to her from that very spot. "Honey! I'm home!"

Well, first things first, the world would have to turn black and white and she looked like hell in a pair of pumps. "I don't even own pearls."

Rock came to a sudden stop at the table. "Pearls?"

She shook her head. "Don't mind me. My brain is slowly frying with all of this time off."

His smile lifted her spirits, a welcome change to her mood from the night before. "Turn on the AC. These units are insulated. I can't wait to walk around here in the summer in sweats."

Rock in sweats.

She would totally be okay with that.

"Hey, better sit down and eat before this food gets cold."

Food.

That got her attention. And her stomach's too. It growled like a mountain cat on the prowl.

"Wow," she laughed, "totally ladylike."

With a grin, he pulled the top off the recyclable container and gave her a wink. "I like a woman who eats. And I think you'll like this."

The plate he set on the table before her chair made her mouth water. "Where did you find this?"

Rock opened a smaller container and set it down.

Kate sank onto the chair and stared at the plate, chewing on her lips.

"Give me a second to get-"

"Right here." Kate reached out and picked up the stack of napkins and silverware. With her eyes still on the plate she managed to separate things so they each had a set. "I didn't know what you were bringing so I brought out everything."

She wanted to wait until he sat down before digging in, but he waved her on.

"Go on, Kate. Dig in. I'll join you in a minute."

He headed into the kitchen and washed his hands at the sink, making quick work of it. When he got back to the table, he stopped beside her. "You waited?"

Kate turned her head to look up at him with a smile. "It's only fair, right? We should eat together."

Some kind of emotion passed over his features, too quick for her to catch it, but something had been there.

And before she could figure out what, if anything, to say, Rock set a hand down on the back of her chair, the other on the edge of the table, and leaned in for a kiss.

It wasn't a hungry kiss, but she swore she could feel passion just under the surface. And yet it wasn't a chaste kiss either. As he pulled back, she felt the tip of his tongue trace the seam of her lips. Before she could chase it with her own, he stood up and moved to his chair.

"Where did you find etouffee?"

His smile made him look more delicious than the food. "I drove past it last week and looked it up online. Courtney's Country Kitchen. I've got biscuits and sausage gravy, and you've got grits in that other container."

She was already lifting a forkful of etouffee to her mouth. "You're trying to make me fat, right?"

"I'm trying to feed you, Kate. Eat."

She did.

And somehow, they managed to have easy conversation as they finished their meals. That's when things shifted between them.

Kate felt Rock's gaze settle on her face a little too

intently and her reaction was just another indication of how confused she was about all of this. She got to her feet with him only a split second behind her. Damn his good manners.

She refused to look him in the face at the moment, reaching for his plate to start cleaning up instead. What a perfect way to delay the conversation she knew they had to have.

But knowing something is going to happen isn't the same as wanting it to happen.

She didn't even manage to lift the plate from the surface of the table before his hand wrapped around hers.

"Leave it, Kate." She felt his thumb sweep over the back of her hand and the gentle touch kicked her heart into gear, bringing it up to racing tempo. "Most of it's just going to get thrown in the trash. I think it's time we have that talk."

He took a step around the small round table and came to a stop in front of her, his big boots a few inches away from her bare toes.

"I thought you wanted this too, Katie."

Her chin tipped up and she met his darkening eyes with her own. "Wanted this? What do you mean?"

She saw the slight narrowing of his eyes and she couldn't blame him. It had to sound like she was trying to put this off.

"This uncertainty," she clarified. "I've drawn the line between us from day one, Rock. And we agreed on it."

He dropped his chin and nodded, his eyes never leaving her face. "I did. It worked for me then. I got to have my hands all over you and my dick inside you."

She couldn't argue with that. "Thank goodness for those mandatory health screenings at work because one look at what you had in your jeans," her smile twisted into a smirk. "I didn't want anything between us."

With the look burning in his eyes, she suspected that he was remembering that first time. And then the second just a few minutes after.

For a man with as much silver as he had in his hair, Rock was still in his prime as far as sex went. She had no complaints.

None. At. All.

"And now," his eyes softened a little, "I feel like we've had this wall between us, Kate. And it hurts. More than I thought it could."

"It's easier," she explained, "when we know the parameters. When we know what our parts are in this... in this..."

"Relationship?" She heard the slight bite in his tone.

"Agreement," she corrected. "Then there's nothing to come between us."

He shook his head. "Then maybe we can talk about why you came down to the fire yesterday."

Her shoulders tensed and her indrawn breath was more of a gasp. "It was an impulse."

She'd blurted out the words, but her expression and the lack of conviction in her tone told him she didn't even believe herself.

Rock reached out and put a hand on her shoulder, gently turning her toward the sitting area just a few feet away.

Since she'd arrived the day before, Kate gravitated to the loveseat. The way it fit into the floorplan and amongst the other chairs in the room gave her a beautiful view of the river bend area. She sat down on the right side and Rock settled in beside her on the other cushion. He laid his arm on the back of the chair and waited for her to speak.

She should start.

After all, she'd driven through town to get to him. The least she could do was try to get him to understand what she was feeling inside and why she was struggling with it.

"Did I ever tell you about my dad?" She drew in a deep, long breath and let it slowly out again. "My dad before he met Cora?"

Rock shook his head. "Not really." He thought on it for a moment and amended his comment. "You call your stepmother Cora. Not Mom. Mama?"

"Walker and Roan are my step-brothers. Their mother and my dad, they married a few years ago out of the blue."

She saw the look of concern in his eyes and knew he was probably reacting to her own jumbled emotions.

My dad was a cheat for most of his life." She cringed. "I hope that's not still true. He says he's not, but I don't know if I can believe him. After all," she fought to keep her tone even, "he cheated on my mother until she couldn't take it anymore."

"She left him." He wasn't posing a question. He was good at reading the signs perhaps.

"I can't seem to remember who left who. When I was young it seemed like one or the other would storm out, angry about something the other one had done or said, and I was kind of the default.

"I came with the house."

She smiled as the words came out of her mouth.

"And when my mom... when she passed on... I ended up with my dad. And his next girlfriend, and the one after that, and his next wife and... on and on." She took a steadying breath and felt Rock's hand settle on her shoulder, his thumb gently brushing back and forth along her collar bone. "When I was old enough to leave, I did. I had to.

"By that point, my dad was in a downward spiral and I couldn't stand seeing him with another one-night stand creeping out of his bedroom." Kate shook herself, trying to break free of the doldrums. "I don't know what changed between the day I left and when my dad found me to tell me that he was getting married one more time." She smiled but it was a brittle gesture. "I thought he was insane, but he invited me to the wedding. That was a first. And he introduced me to my brothers."

"No one thinks that you're just step-siblings," he told her. "The three of you are family."

She smiled and nodded. "Although, the next time Walker calls me his 'older' sister, I think we might be down to two sibs instead of three."

They both chuckled at the idea, but the soft sounds of their laughter faded away eventually.

"From what I could see. From what I hear... Cora is good for my dad and he's... he's good to her. I pray it stays that way, but the little girl inside of me is just waiting for Cora to come to her senses and become yet another ex-stepmom."

Kate felt tears coming and closed her eyes, hoping beyond hope that the feeling would disappear. The last thing she wanted to do was be weak in Rock's eyes.

"Are you saying that you don't want to be in a relationship with me because you think I'm going to cheat on you? Or maybe that I'm just going to be an ass and walk away because I'm going to tire of you?"

She lifted her chin, ready to defend her answer. "Maybe I am! Or maybe I think I'm going to be the one to mess things up. I share his DNA, not you! What if everything's going along, right as rain, married, kids, and then one of us is ready to move on?"

"Kate," his fingertips brushed against her temple, "Your mom didn't just move on. She died, Kate. She-"

"My dad, okay? I think it's him that I hate so much and yet, I worry that I'm too much like him for your own good. I'm trying to save you from being stuck with me only to find out that it changes along the way." She looked around at the room. "What happens when you realize that maybe the best part of knowing me is just the sex?" She was almost seething when she stopped, her shoulders rising and falling in frustration. "I can't do this to you, Rock. I can't."

"I'm okay with this, Kate. I'm in love with you and I'm going to love you no matter what. I'm old enough and set in my ways enough to know that what I feel for you is right."

"Rock," she shook her head. "It's the chase. Maybe you think I'm playing hard to get and that just makes this appealing somehow? I just don't think we can go from fuck buddies to romance. And if we did, what happens when it's time to turn back and we both get really hurt."

"Kate." He shifted closer on the seat until his shoulder bumped up against her. "I'm in this. I'm willing to take the chance that you'll hurt me. I'm willing to do it because I think you won't do that to me. Sure, we'll have misunderstandings and arguments, but who doesn't.

"Not to mention the make-up sex. I know that's going to be so damn good between us."

She sighed and dropped her chin down to her chest. "You make it sound so simple."

"That's because it is, Kate." The tone of Rock's voice, the look in his eyes, seemed to goad her to keep talking. "It's that simple. I love you. I want to be with you. I just need to know if you're going to take that chance and be with me."

When she didn't reply she wondered how he'd react. She expected a wall. A cold front to come between them. She expected a fight. And maybe a slammed door or two. That's how things were dealt with between her parents. That was the next logical, illogical step.

"Can you try, Kate? Do you even want to see what it might be like sharing more of our lives than just sex? More of our lives than just the anguish of the job. Maybe we can celebrate the good too. And when it comes to the rest of it, be there for each other."

"I can try." Those words almost killed her. Honest was one thing. Hopeful? That was damn scary. "I can try this... this relationship with you." She could feel the cold sweat on her forehead, the clammy skin on her palms. "But it's not going to be as easy as you seem to think," she gave him a dark and searching look, "it's not about if I can love you, Rock."

This, she wondered, *was what it was like to stand on a cliff, ready to jump.*

The cliff, she decided, would be so much easier than this conversation.

And there he was, sitting there, so damn patient with her.

She didn't deserve him.

Not by a long shot.

But he did deserve the truth, even if there was a chance that he might not like it.

"Kate, baby-"

"I think I already do."

Kate felt something turn inside of her. Like a key twisting in an old lock, it moved the tumblers, but it didn't open.

Yet.

He held himself still, watching.

Waiting.

"Why do I hear a 'but' in that."

Breathe.

No, really, breathe!

"That's because I'm not sure if it's enough."

Wide-eyed and so damn gorgeous, Rock leaned closer, his hand gently covering her knee. "It's more than enough, Kate. I can work with that. We can work with that."

She fought off tears, hating to look vulnerable.

Hating to feel it too.

"It doesn't solve a thing for us," she shook her head and continued, "it just means that when it's over, I don't think I'll ever move past it. Move past us."

"Then we don't let it end. We hold on tight. We make it work."

"I can still hear my mom crying herself to sleep." Her eyes drifted closed and she fought to push the memories away, but they just crowded in on her. "I can hear it inside my head, like an echo that just won't stop."

"I love you, Kate."

The aching sobs in her head receded.

She felt Rock's hands on her, turning her toward him.

She felt a kiss on her cheek and then on her lips. Just a soft, tender brush of his lips.

"I love you, Kate."

A shiver rolled through her when she felt his beard against the underside of her jaw and tilted her head to give him more access.

"I love you... and that's never going to change."

His kisses continued down her neck and then along her shoulder. The sleep shirt that Pilar had brought over the night before fell from Kate's shoulder and she felt Rock lean his head against her chest as he wrapped his arms around her middle.

She held him there, her hands pressed against his head, the ends of his hair tickling her palms.

His breath feathered across her nipple through the cotton fabric and she felt it harden, followed a moment later by its twin.

Rock drew in a breath and smiled, his eyes still closed. "I can hear your heart beating, Kate. Strong. True." He rubbed his cheek against her chest and his nose brushed along the inside curve of her breast. "Just like mine, baby. Let me love you. Let me show you that being together isn't something to be afraid of."

Her heart stuttered in her chest. She felt it rush right back into rhythm in the next moment. And then it started to pound. Pushing blood through her body, making her tingle all over.

"I don't want... I don't want to be afraid. But, I am."

He leaned back and looked her straight in the eye. "I'll protect your heart, Katie. I can do that. You don't have to do everything on your own. Not anymore. Not ever again."

He saw the doubt flicker in her eyes. He knew Kate well enough that he didn't miss that sign. He saw that fear in her too.

Lord knows he was afraid too.

Afraid to lose her.

"Come with me, Katie."

He got up off of the loveseat and held out his hand.

It took a moment, but she set her hand in his and let him bring her up onto her feet.

In less than a dozen steps they were inside his bedroom and he drew up short.

Kate stepped up beside him, her hand warming in his. "Sorry, I didn't get a chance to make the bed, I over-"

He picked her up and pulled her in for a kiss. He swallowed her gasp of surprise before his tongue slipped between her lips to tangle with hers.

When he set her down, she looked up at him in shock, flat on her back in his bed.

He looked down at her, his eyes traveling over her body from head to toe and back again. "Do you have any idea what it does to me knowing that you slept in my bed last night?"

Her gaze lowered from his face and he felt his cock twitch in his jeans like it wanted to preen for her. Wanted to be touched by her.

He felt the same damn way.

She swallowed and he watched the way her muscles moved under her skin. "I think I have some idea."

"Which side?" His voice was lower, deeper as his lungs worked to bring air into his body. He licked his lips. "Which side did you sleep on?"

Sheepishly, she reached out her arm and gave the bed a pat with her open hand. "This side."

A growl rolled out of his throat. "That's my side."

Her cheeks pinked and her lips curled up in a little smile. "Okay, sorry."

Rock stepped forward and she parted her knees enough to let him step between her legs. "Don't be." He reached up behind him and peeled his t-shirt off. "We can share."

Her indrawn breath was almost a sigh. "I like that idea."

He smiled.

How could he do anything else?

Reaching down he undid the buttons on his jeans and grunted when the pressure on his dick eased. He shoved his jeans down before remembering he had his boots on.

"Fuck."

Her soft laughter didn't do a thing to dampen his arousal. He bent down and made quick work of his laces and when he looked up, he couldn't help the silly grin on his face.

"You were busy."

Kate looked at him, her teeth worrying her bottom lip as she dangled her boy short panties from her big toe. "Thought I'd give you a hand."

He plucked it from her and tossed it onto the small pile of clothes beside him and slid that hand up her inner thigh. "I'd like to get my hands on you."

Her lips parted on a moan. "Yes, please."

His grin was almost feral, his skin tingling at the sound of her words. "Are you begging me?"

"Asking." Her eyes were full of challenge. "I know what I want."

He nodded his head and slipped his fingers between her folds, feeling the caress of her heat and the silken curls of her sex. "I'd beg to get inside of you, Katie. I'd beg if it meant I'd get to fuck you senseless."

She smiled and stretched against the rumpled sheets of his bed and his cock felt like it was going to explode. "You don't have to beg, Rock. You just have to give it to me."

Rock looked down at her and saw a lightness in her expression that he'd never seen before. Felt the glorious heat of her thighs against his skin. If he didn't get inside of her soon, he was going to lose it and paint himself all over her skin.

That, he reasoned, could always happen later, but for now.

He leaned forward and grabbed her hips, pulling her toward the edge of the bed before he let them go. The angle of his hips rubbed his cock against her, and her eyes rolled.

"Well," she sighed and arched her lower back, rubbing herself against the hard length of his shaft, "that answers my question."

"What question?" He just had to know.

When she looked into his eyes, her cheeks and chest pink with arousal, she lowered her gaze to his cock. "Why you bought a bed this high."

Sliding his hands around to the backs of her thighs, just beneath her butt, he lifted just a little and rolled his hips against her. "I bought it for us."

Her body tensed against him, her eyes wide open and fixed on him. "Really?"

Rock smoothed his hands over her thighs, up and down until he held her in just the right way. He curled his hips and let his cock ride along her folds and her clit.

Kate dropped her forearm across her mouth, and he heard the muffled sound of her voice.

Smiling, he shook his head.

"The two sisters who live on this floor are all but deaf, Katie. You don't have to be quiet."

She smiled back. "Well, then you're going to have to see how loud, I can ge- oh god yes!"

He sank into her, all the way to the hilt, and had to stop to catch his breath.

She'd drained it right out of him with the tight fit of her pussy.

When he'd pulled himself together enough to speak, he looked down into her beautiful face. "Hard or gentle,

Katie?" He felt her inner walls clench and relax against him. "Hard? Or gentle?"

To answer him, she tugged at the hem of her sleep shirt and as she arched to pull it off, she canted her hips and drew a long, guttural groan from his lips.

She smiled as she lifted her hands and cupped her hands over her breasts, letting her hardened nipples peek out from between her fingers. With a sigh, she gave him a little show, pinching her nipples and wiggling against him. "Give me everything, Rock. I want you."

He swore he felt his cock harden even more inside of her. The silken grip of her walls and the liquid heat of her arousal was going to tie him up in knots.

And he was going to love every damn minute.

"Hold on to those," he nodded toward her breasts, "I'm going to want to taste them later."

A soft sound escaped her parted lips. "Yes..."

Rock knew they hadn't solved all of their problems. Hell, they'd just scratched the surface.

But he was going to love Kate in every way he could until they figured it out.

Just like this. He filled his hands with the taut globes of her ass and started to fuck her with everything he had.

[13]

ROCK & KATE

Kate felt her stomach take another drop on her emotional roller coaster.

From her seat on Rock's sofa, she grabbed at his hand and held on for dear life. "I can't look. I can't look."

"There's nothing for you to look at... yet."

She heard his soft laughter and dug what little fingernails she had into his skin.

His indrawn breath was her momentary reward.

From the makeshift control room on Rock's dinner table, Irish Healey, 9-1-1 operator, was in her element. "Raffe? Do you have the Douche in your sights?"

Douche had become Irish's go-to nickname for Doug Fitchett. And when Irish said the word, she constantly found new ways to pronounce and enunciate it.

A voice came through one of the many speakers and screens that Irish had set up when she came over a few hours before.

"Yep. Still on course."

Kate tensed and Rock dropped his arm over her shoulders.

"Breathe."

She nodded but didn't quite manage a breath. The big plan had been underway for the better part of an hour. And so far, the volunteers from House Twenty-Nine had trailed Doug... Douche... from his work to his apartment. And then he'd stepped back out on the street and hopped into a car parked at the curb.

Raffe, one of the EMTs that worked out of Twenty-Nine was the first car to pick up his trail from there.

She knew there were at least two other cars in the area, all spaced apart to catch him when he left. They were now moving to nearby streets waiting to pick up the trail when Irish called for the switch.

Rock leaned down and brushed a kiss along the edge of her ear, tickling her. "She's kind of scary."

Kate slid a sideways look at Irish who looked like a space-age commander on a battle cruiser. The blue light on her face clashed with the pink in her hair making it look almost neon with the contrast. Leaning back against him she nodded slowly.

Another voice called through the open comm. "I see him coming my way, I'm at a stop sign, waiting to turn on... to..."

Irish already had a map up on the screen and her hot pink fingernail was following the glowing red dot. "Freeman. Yes. Okay, Russell, take the turn- and pick-up Douche boy when he passes you. Raffe, take a convenient side street and head toward the interstate."

"Yes, Captain, my Captain!"

Kate saw Irish sit up a little straighter in her chair and looked into the screen with a proud grin. "You got that right, Raffe. Remind my cousin of that the next time you see him, okay?"

Raffe's laugh was almost a snort through the speaker. "Yes, ma'am."

Kate hissed. "Ohh... he better watch that ma'am thing."

Irish covered her microphone and looked at her. "Right?"

Kate's phone blipped and she picked it up. A call from SERENA CAMPOS.

Getting up from the couch, she walked to the far side of the room before answering the call. "Hey."

"Do I want to know what your friends are up to?"

Her friends. It felt odd to hear it said, but it really was true. Her friends. "It's still going on right now. Do you want me to tell you what's happening?"

"No. Nope. Definitely not!" Serena's laugh was a little brittle. "I have to say that I'm more than a little worried about how this is going to shake out. You do realize that if it doesn't go the way your brother and his friend planned, you might be in more trouble in regards to this lawsuit?"

Kate nodded even though Serena couldn't see it. "I know. I really do. I just feel like what they have planned might just tip the scales in my favor. There are no guarantees. I know that. Believe me, I do. But I've got a whole slew of wonderful people trying to make this happen.

"They know the rules about what they can and cannot do. I have faith in these people."

"Okay. I hear you."

Kate heard Serena mumble a few prayers in Spanish under her breath. Kate only knew a few words of the language, but she recognized some of the wording that Pilar used when she was frustrated. It was almost enough to make her laugh but she held back. She didn't want to tempt fate.

"Call me when it's over and we'll figure out where to go from there. Crossing my fingers for you, Kate."

She looked over at Rock and he was watching her from his place on the couch. The smile he gave her made her melt. How crazy was it that she was opening herself to the prospect of a relationship, just when her life could be imploding?

"I'll call you, Serena. I think we'll both have a really good night."

"I like that positive attitude, Kate. Hold onto that. Bye!"

The call ended before Kate could reply back. She lowered the phone from her ear and saw that Rock was still watching her. The look in his eyes made her feel like the most beautiful and the most powerful woman in the world. She couldn't lose when he looked at her like that.

She walked back to the couch and sat down beside him, leaning into his embrace.

"Everything okay?"

She nodded. "It will be. Did I miss anything?"

Rock reached forward and slipped his fingers between hers and held her hand. "I was missing you."

A ping sounded from one of Irish's speakers. "Speak and ye shall be heard!"

"Hey, Irish. This is Kennedy Heart."

Irish's voice changed a little, softening. "Reporting about Center City from the Heart. You're on the air in more than one way, Kennedy."

Waving at Kate, Irish gestured toward one of the screens. Getting back up, Kate didn't let go of Rock's hand and the two of them moved in behind the dining table and watched as a strange camera angle was focused on a building. The half-dark backlit sign above the front door spelled out TAP THAT.

"Kennedy. When you get inside remember that we have three guys in there who have your back. So, if anything happens and someone grabs your hand. You go, okay?"

A soft whisper of a laugh could be heard. "Not my first rodeo, but thanks."

Kate and Irish shared a look. They both remembered when they saw the picture that Kennedy sent them before she left her apartment and got into the ride share to take her to Tap That, just southeast of Interstate Ninety-Two.

The well-worn and baggy 'boyfriend' jeans made Kennedy look almost twenty pounds heavier and matching her bulky gray sweatshirt with the Blue and Black Cyclones Hockey logo on it. Her beat up baseball hat was embroidered with the BREWERS logo across the front. She'd looked ready to head into any dive bar in that area of town. It wasn't until the second photo that Kate wondered if they should call off the whole thing. The text before the picture was complete with a smiley face at the end.

> KH: *Sorry for the delay. Took me a while to get wired up.*

The picture showed Kennedy holding up the hem of her sweatshirt to show them what was underneath. If Kate didn't know better, she would think the perky red head was walking around with some kind of technologically advanced bomb strapped to her chest.

That was an image that was going to give her nightmares.

For weeks.

"Where the hell did she get all of that equipment? Is this sanctioned by the Station?"

Irish explained, "I have a friend in an improv group that

posts videos on YouTube." Irish grinned and pointed to the Center City Cyclones Puck Pin on Kennedy's sweatshirt in the first photo. "This is a camera that works like a body cam."

Kate sighed as she looked longingly at the little device. "If I get back on the force. I don't think I'm going to wait for the City Council to get the budget for them, I'm going to buy one of those and videotape when I'm on the street."

"When you get back, Kate." Rock put his hands on her hips and she instinctively leaned back against him.

Now, firmly rooted in the present, Kate's eyes acclimated to the bounce and sway of Kennedy's body easily enough. She felt Rock's hands settle on her hips as they watched. Kennedy's arm extended and she pushed open the door.

As soon as she was inside they saw her hand reach down and although they couldn't see everything, Kate had a feeling that Kennedy was wiping her palm on the leg of her jeans. "That door is filthy," Kennedy grumbled under her breath. "Yuck."

Irish hunched over the desk and opened up a bunch of extra browser windows on her screens.

Kate set a hand on the desk to steady herself and looked at the individual windows.

"How did you get their security feed?"

Irish kept her gaze directed at the screen ahead of her. "It's not exactly legal, so I don't think we can use any of this footage to help you, but it's all part of that favor I asked my gaming friend."

Kate nodded. "The one who altered the coding on the

map locator app so we could use it to track everyone in real time?"

"One and the same," Irish announced with pride. "He hacked into their cameras for me so I could see inside. Kennedy's little camera is only going to help with the immediate problem. If anything else happens, we'll need a wider view to get her out of there safely."

Rock leaned against Kate's back and she couldn't help but lean into his warmth as he perused the feed along with her. "Irish, has anyone told you that you're scary good with this stuff?"

"Not really," her voice was a little hushed, "I don't break out these skills on a normal day, especially because it's not exactly sanctioned by Law Enforcement. So here I am using my super stealthy skills to bring justice to the world! Or," she grinned at them, "my corner of the world. Oh, look here."

Irish used the end of her glittering stylus to point at the upper left box.

"See that guy? The one in the plaid shirt and unfortunate hairstyle?"

Kate followed the end of the stylus and nodded. "Yes."

"That's Russell Web."

Rock chuckled. "I told him to cut that shag on his head."

Irish shrugged. "It works for this."

She pointed out a few other people in the room. Kate smiled. This was the backup that Irish had told Kennedy to expect.

Still, Kate worried. Doug Pritchett struck her as a man who didn't like to have his ego challenged. If he figured out what Kennedy was doing, he probably wouldn't react well.

Ah hell, who was she kidding? He was an ass. He'd

already beat his wife. What would stop him from striking out at Kennedy.

"Irish, maybe we should call this off."

"Shh... look."

Gesturing at the screen that showed the feed from the pin camera, Irish sat forward, her hands poised and ready. When the camera held steady for a moment, they all took a breath. And then the height of the camera lowered and sitting just along the side of the image, was Doug Pritchett. He was holding court at a table with two pitchers on the table. One, almost empty and the other had a full head of foam.

Irish pressed a button and whispered into her microphone. "Okay folks pay attention. This is it."

Kennedy Heart sat down with a bottle of beer in her hand, careful to keep it out of the range of the camera. It was crazy loud in the room, but she'd already done a few tests of the microphone and recording system with Irish using her sister's stereo. The directional microphone was sensitive enough to pick up a conversation even with Nickelback pounding through the air. It was going to pick up whatever Doug was saying to his nasty friends.

Her heart was pounding in her chest so hard she worried that it might drown out the voices in the recording. She forced herself to sit back in her chair and try to look normal.

It wasn't easy.

She'd kind of misrepresented how often she'd done undercover reporting like this.

Okay, she'd lied about it.

The closest thing she'd done to going undercover for a story was when she was in Junior High School and she'd purposefully said something rude to her teacher to get herself assigned to detention. All that got her was the silent treatment from her parents and two weeks of picking up trash on the playground. Total failure.

This... this was going to be better. Irish Healey was a freaking magician, and she was going to be a huge help in the future.

Turning her head toward the back door she could almost hear a few words of their conversation. She hoped that Irish was having more luck hearing it.

Maybe if she leaned a little closer-

"Take a drink."

She had to lean back as someone passed right by her nose and slumped into the chair beside hers.

The nerve!

"I said, take a drink."

Ready to tell this jerk exactly where to step off, Kennedy turned and stopped short.

"Detec-"

"Here, I'll show you how."

Detective Walker Ashley reached out and yanked the bottle of beer from her hand and took a drink from it. Then he leaned closer and stared at her. "You come into a bar, you order a drink, and then you drink the drink."

She snatched it back and took a sip, trying to ignore the thought that his lips had been there already. "I know how to drink."

He snorted. "Right. Now take another."

Kennedy narrowed her eyes at him. She didn't like pushy guys.

But she took a drink anyway.

His answering smile was disgusting.

"Jerk."

He shrugged and waved at a passing waitress who almost tripped over her own feet to make a beeline for their table. He ordered a beer and winked at the woman, sending her off in a cloud of smoke from the other patrons.

"Why are you here?" She kept the position of her head away from the directional microphone. "I'm doing this alone."

"You think I'm going to let you do this crappy of a job at undercover and that I'm not going to help?"

"I didn't ask you."

"I didn't ask you either," he grumbled, "but since you're helping my sister then I'm going to do you a solid right back. So, shut up and let's get this over with so I can take you out for a good, stiff drink."

She felt her cheeks heat.

Good, stiff…

Yeah, her mind went there.

Went down. There.

You know.

Oh god, she was going to lose her mind.

Focus, Kennedy! Focus!

"I'm so not going out with you."

She didn't know why she continued to talk.

"Okay, so we can have the drink here," he winked, "but I'm thinking they might not like you after you expose Doug's stupidity."

She took another long pull on the beer bottle and she leaned forward to hiss at him.

"Which I won't be able to hear if you keep talking."

A disembodied voice echoed in her head. "Come on,

you two. Let's get this over with and then you can save this flirty foreplay for later."

"Flirty?" Walker sneered at the idea.

"Foreplay?" Kennedy shuddered visible, but there were parts of her that tingled at the thought.

"Okay...." Irish dragged the word out like she didn't believe their shock and outrage.

Kennedy didn't mind because she didn't believe it either.

"Sending in the cavalry."

Someone in dirty, well-worn boots stumbled up to Doug's table and clapped a hand down on his shoulder. "I know you."

Doug's expression said, 'Fuck off.' His words said something else. "So what?"

"You're that guy... you know," leaning heavily on the table, the man turned to look around the room and Kennedy drew in a startled breath, "isn't that-"

The detective grabbed her hand in his and held tight. "No one you know, sweetheart."

She got the point. She wasn't stupid.

Just shocked. Okay?

She looked at the man standing at the table and realized where she'd seen him before. At the fire station. It made sense. You need someone to have your back, go with family. The kind of family that people chose. That was the good stuff.

"You were in the news, right?"

Doug's expression was downright dangerous. Kennedy wanted to say something. She wanted to warn the firefighter to be careful. Doug might not understand what he was talking about.

Walker must have seen her intent, because he held her

hand so tightly against the tabletop that she was afraid her wrist would be stuck there when she tried to lift it away.

Looking the man over, Doug lifted his chin, daring him to cross the line. "What the hell man!"

Russell Webb, yes, that was his name. Young, blond, muscled for days.

Russell held up his hands in a gesture meant to placate Doug. "Sorry, man. I was just going to buy you and your friends a round of shots."

"Shots?" Now he had Doug's attention. "Why?"

Leaning in closer, Russell let out a little chuckle. "'Cause you're takin' that pig to court. Suin' her ass!"

Russell didn't wait for the okay, he just lifted his hand and caught sight of a server. "Hey. Can I get a round for my friends here?"

When the round of shots came, Russell paid for it and made a toast to Doug.

Kennedy wanted to wash her ears out with soap. It was bad enough that some male officers had such a hate on for women officers. As women they faced a lot of horrible things in society.

Maybe it was what Russell had said to the man. Or maybe it was the alcohol, but in just a few minutes, Doug was mouthing off. And he did it loud enough that someone across the bar could have heard, even without a microphone.

The more he talked about how he was going to 'take the bitch for everything she's worth' the more other things slipped out. The way he'd lied his way through the medical exam for his neck pain after she took him down, to the way he'd 'kicked the shit out of' his wife for making him look like an ass. And finally, Doug had swallowed a huge glass of beer in one long gulp and told the bar, "Hell, when she loses her job for good, she'll have to find a way to pay me off." His smile was more of a sloppy smirk. "I'll let her do it on her knees."

Cat calls and other vulgar words were called out.

Kennedy's fingers were white knuckling it around the bottle. "That asshole."

Walker leaned closer and gripped their joined hands together. Holding her in place. "Let it go."

She turned on him. "I can't believe you. You can't just let him get away with that."

Walker looked down at her Cyclones Puck Pin and smiled at her. "We won't. Now let's get out of here."

She hesitated when he stood up and the harried waitress who was walking through the crowd with a full tray of glasses, all but collided with Kennedy.

"Sorry," Kennedy murmured, but the older woman waved it off.

"It happens."

Kennedy turned to Walker, ready to leave after that near miss, but somehow, they'd drawn the attention of someone else in the room.

"You're that reporter!"

Doug apparently watched Channel Twelve.

Kennedy heard Irish's voice in her ear. "Go, Kennedy. What are you waiting for?"

Walker tugged on her arm and Kennedy started to follow him, but suddenly Doug was reaching between them, keeping her from leaving.

"What the hell are you doing in here, huh? Slumming with us, Princess?"

She lifted her chin and looked him straight in the eye. "I'm leaving, Mr. Pritchett. And I would appreciate it if you let me go."

Doug and his intoxicated friends were starting to laugh in short, punctuated snorts of sound. "Woman, the only thing I'm going to let you do is put your mouth around my-"

She watched in horror as Doug's head snapped back and blood drops flew in a disturbingly slow arc over his head.

"Ow!" She hissed and looked down at her hand, only to realize that it was hurting because she'd just punched him in the face with it. "I can't believe I did that."

Before she could even begin to figure out what to do, Walker pulled her out of a side door and hustled her down the sidewalk and through a few sketchy looking alleys. He didn't even stop when she worried about someone jumping them in the dark. He just kept walking and dragging her with him.

They only stopped when they got to a black SUV parked in the pool of light created by a rather anemic streetlamp. He used the key fob in his pocket to unlock the passenger door. He held it open when she got inside the car.

It was only when she thought better of getting into his vehicle that she saw a dangerous glint in his eyes. "I can call a ride share company."

He dropped his chin to give her a look that said she was a few apples short of a bushel. "Do you see any open businesses out here?"

She didn't even have to look. She just glared right back at him. "No."

"I'm not going to waste time sitting around and waiting for you to come to your senses. Let's go."

Lord help her she just couldn't stop herself. "You can't just order me around, you know."

His laughter was almost silent. "I can."

She drew back, glaring at him. "No, you can't."

"Damn it, Kennedy."

Before she could say another word, Detective Walker Ashley grabbed her chin and kissed her.

He kissed her really, really well.

Goodness.

As promised, Serena Campos did indeed lose her mind when she heard about all the drama that happened at the bar. Then again, she did laugh when she saw the video of Doug Pritchett falling onto his ass after a woman cracked him in the face for vulgar language.

The news cycle was going to be a circus for the next few days. Kate didn't even need to be told that. It was just how stories like this worked.

The news played the video of Doug talking about how he was setting Kate up on a bogus claim of brutality. The video brought a lot of things into question, including possible fraud on his behalf by his so-called doctors.

Not to mention when Detective Walker Ashley arrested WCCN's newest sensation, Kennedy Heart for assault and then walked her through her arraignment and put up the bail money himself.

Kate and Rock had only left his place to go down to City Hall and have the Mayor explain that she'd been cleared of all charges and the civil lawsuit had been dropped. And Captain Catalano had been there to inquire when she'd be coming back to the department, as if her suspension had been a voluntary vacation.

She'd looked him right in the eye and told him she'd be back in a week and then they'd gone back to his apartment and Rock had stripped her bare and made love to her while he was waiting on his own last-minute request for a few days off.

Things were changing inside of her. The events of the last few weeks had brought that realization home. What had left her satisfied a few months ago paled in comparison to what she wanted now.

Rock? Oh, he was giving it to her.

In so many delicious and satisfying ways.

There was just one last hurdle that they had to jump through before things could settled down again.

And it was a doozy.

[14]

ROCK & KATE

Rock pulled up to the valet stand at Gabrielle's and with a quick hand gesture asked the young man in a red suit coat for a moment. When he turned to look at Kate, he found her staring straight out of the windshield, her hands folded in her lap.

It might have looked to anyone else that she was just taking a moment to compose herself, but Rock noticed the tight set of her jaw and the white visible around her knuckles. She might look calm, but Kate was struggling to look that way.

He reached over and covered her hands with one of his. He swept his thumb back and forth over her skin and noticed that it was a little cold and clammy. Not something he associated with Kate at all. She could face down angry men taller and heavier than she was, but having dinner with her family? Not so much.

"Have I told you how beautiful you are?"

His voice seemed to shock her a little, but it didn't get much of a reaction.

"You're just saying that to make me feel better."

Rock's eyebrow lifted a little. "I think that's kind of my job, babe, but you know I love the way you look."

She gave him a sideways look. "You love me naked."

He couldn't help but chuckle at that. "You know it. But I also like you in clothes too."

It was her turn to raise a brow at that.

"It just means that I get to take them off of you later."

Color rose in her cheeks and her lips softened from the pale line they'd been most of the drive to the restaurant. "You know I'm perfectly capable of taking them off on my own."

He lifted a shoulder and made a little contemplative sound before he spoke. "Sure, you can. But that doesn't mean you have to. I'm a helpful guy."

"Helpful." Her snort was followed by a soft chuckle of her own. "Is that what you call it."

Her hands had loosened enough for him to separate them, saving him the work of prying them apart. He linked his fingers through the hand closest to him and leaned in toward her. "What would you call it?"

She took her first noticeable breath, her shoulders rising slightly before dropping down again. "I call it getting handsy, Mr. Ferris."

The sly smile that touched his lips made her smile in turn.

"I'll get handsy with you anytime you want, Katie. Just say the word."

She turned slightly on the bench seat of his truck and the movement revealed just the hint of leg to his gaze. He knew he'd been caught when she laughed. "The eyes are up here."

He let his thumb graze over her covered thigh. "And I'll be staring into those eyes tonight when I'm deep inside you,

Kate. Don't forget that. No matter what happens, we have each other."

Yeah, she was just about to tell him to turn the car around when someone knocked on the passenger window.

Kate turned to look and saw Walker staring in like a Peeping Tom, one hand cupped around his eyes.

Before she could do anything, Rock reached across her lap and flipped him off.

Laughing, she looked back at Rock. "I could have done that."

"I know," he shrugged, "but I'm always happy to flip off your annoying brother."

Kate laughed out loud at that. "Let's get out so Walker can annoy the family as a whole."

He let out a breath that he'd been holding onto. Walker was an acquired taste for him. Like castor oil. He'd take it, but he wasn't sure he wanted it.

Opening his door, he looked back at Kate who was still glaring at her brother. Chuckling to himself he got out, tossed the keys to the eager valet, and walked around to the passenger door.

"Move it, Walker. You're blocking the door."

With his hands held up in mock surrender, Walker stepped back, and Rock was able to open the door for Kate. He held out a hand to help her and smiled when she took it.

Since the day they'd cleared the air between them and Kate had trusted him enough to explain some of her misgivings about relationships, she'd been reaching for him more. Touching him more outside of sex.

It made him feel good, like she trusted him. Or at the least, wanted him to touch her enough to initiate it. She stepped out of the truck and came to a stop beside him. Kate leaned closer and whispered a few words to him.

Rock turned and saw the valet sitting in the driver's seat, but he hadn't yet put the car in gear. The young man looked as if he was staring at a priceless treasure.

Rock laughed softly. "Careful, son. Don't drool on my upholstery."

The valet nodded as if he was in a trance. "Oh, I'll be careful, sir. This truck is the bomb!"

Rock shook his head. "Okay. Thanks. I guess."

When they started walking toward the grand entrance of the building, Kate wound her arm around his and laid her head on his shoulder for a moment.

"You're a good man, Rock."

"What about me?" Walker jogged up beside them. "I'm your favorite brother. It says so in your phone."

Kate's shoulders shook in silent laughter. "You're the one who put that in when I went to the bathroom at the diner!"

Walker shrugged. "You left it that way."

That got a good, honest laugh out of Kate and Rock had to give Walker credit. He wasn't sure if the annoying detective knew about Kate's issues with her dad, but he seemed to be trying to help put Kate in a better mind frame about the dinner ahead and that earned him a few grudging points.

The hostess at the front desk of Gabrielle's made quite the impression on them when she all but salivated over Walker in his suit. So much so that she had to ask them twice for the name of their party before the answer registered on her brain.

"Ah, yes. The Turner Party. We have your table ready for you. This way please."

The poor woman made it across the fine carpeted floor without tripping over her tongue and Rock sighed. He was damn lucky to have Kate beside him.

They approached a table set for eight and a couple was already waiting. Kate slowed her steps a little and Rock easily followed suit, wanting to take his cues from her. The couple stood to greet Walker and he stepped in for a long hug from his mother.

Rock could easily see the resemblance between Walker and his mother. He couldn't exactly put his finger on what it was, but with the two standing near each other, there was no mistaking that they were mother and son.

He resisted the urge to look at Kate and search for a physical resemblance to her father. He could see that they shared some of their coloring, but it seemed like a cursory connection at best. Rock sized up her father and found that they were almost the same height, but her dad was a slight man in body weight. Rock didn't think Kate had ever said what her father did as a profession.

"Kate!" Cora Turner held out her arms for a hug and Kate walked closer to accept it.

Rock saw a pinch between her shoulder blades, tension in the situation, but once Cora had Kate in her arms, that eased out of Kate's body. He could see her relax into her stepmother's embrace easily.

The two women shared a few quiet words and Kate blushed prettily at something Cora said and earned Rock's regard for that gesture.

"Cora, I'd like to introduce you to-" Rock saw Kate hesitate over his name, "Martin Ferris. He's a firefighter at Station House Twenty-Nine. They're a few blocks away from the Precinct."

"Well, hello there, Martin Ferris of Twenty-Nine. That's more words than I've heard about any man from Kate. High praise indeed."

He saw Kate blush again as he stepped forward to shake Cora's hand.

If he thought he'd get away with that, he'd been wrong. Cora grabbed a hold of his upper-arms and drew him in for a hug. "You'll be good to my girl, Mister Ferris, or I'll have the last laugh, you hear?"

He stepped back laughing at her threat. "Yes, Ma'am. I have every intention to be good to Kate. Please, call me Rock, all of my friends do."

Cora turned to look at Kate and mouthed the word 'ROCK' before she waggled her brows and Rock thought Kate might melt into the ground right then and there. Cora poked at his forearms through the suit and then gave his bicep a squeeze. "Goodness, they build you boys like rocks don't they."

Walker groaned something about putting a bullet in his brain to which Cora gave his arm a good swat.

"You know better than to say things like that. Don't invite trouble, Walker."

Kate's brother, the big, bad detective, winced away from his mother's hand. "Hey, it's not about inviting it, Mom. Kate and I work for the police. We're kind of always in the middle of things."

Cora rolled her eyes at Walker's comment and Rock couldn't help but see a resemblance between the two beautiful women, even if it wasn't genetic. Kate had an innate connection to Cora Turner, and it was easy to see.

Cora made the introduction between Rock and her husband and Rock noticed that he didn't walk forward to shake his hand. And he certainly hadn't said a word in greeting to his daughter or tried to show her any affection.

Kate was handling it, but he wasn't sure if she was handling it well. Her smile was a little tight, the lipstick that she'd applied earlier was likely gone from the way she was rubbing her lips together.

"Mom!"

Cora turned when she heard Roan's voice and she rushed forward with a big grin on her face. "Look at you two! So gorgeous!"

As Cora hugged Roan, Kate moved to his side and she looked up at him. "Sorry about my dad. He's... difficult."

The things that he wanted to say to Charles Turner would wait. He didn't want to say anything in front of Kate that would hurt her, but he just couldn't understand how a man like Charles Turner, who seemed to dote on his wife, seemed so cold around his daughter.

"He's really kind of awkward around new people."

Rock nodded out of habit. "What was his profession again?"

Kate cocked her head at the word 'again,' showing him that she'd never told him that detail about her dad, but she didn't call him on it. "He taught. My dad's been a college professor for as long as I can remember. I bet he's glad to be retired."

Rock tried not to react to the words. It was more likely that his students were glad that he retired.

"Charles, come here and meet Pilar."

Kate steeled herself and Rock had a feeling that she was worried about her friend. Sure, Kate was still Pilar's sergeant, but off duty they were becoming close friends as well.

Rock half expected to see Roan take his stepfather to task the instant he held back from greeting his fiancé.

And then the funniest thing happened.

Charles Turner busted out a smile. An honest to god, all the way up to his eye-balls smile. He pulled Pilar in for a hug and as he stepped back, a kiss on each cheek. If Pilar hadn't looked so relieved by the greeting Rock would have been really pissed. As it was, he was just worried about Kate.

He turned to look at her and she had a smile plastered on. Her eyes were too bright. And damn, he felt her holding onto his hand like a lifeline.

He would let her hold onto it as long as she wanted. And later on, he'd do whatever it took to make things right for her. Maybe everyone assumed that because Kate was an officer in charge of others that her emotions weren't as tender as others. It wasn't nice, but who knew the family dynamics at play. And Rock had never had much family to begin with. All he had as clues about how things worked in a family were those old sappy TV shows like *The Waltons*, *Eight is Enough*, hell, even *The Brady Bunch* had some redeeming qualities when it came to family dynamics.

Still, he had a feeling the family he'd joined at the House was a lot more functional than Kate's.

He hoped he was wrong. He really did.

But either way, he was going to let Kate know that he considered her family, and he wasn't going to let her fall by the wayside, ever.

Halfway through the meal, Kate was trying to decide if dessert was worth it. Oh, she'd seen a number of write-ups about the pastry chef at Gabrielle's and she had a particular weakness for anything that sounded French in its name. It usually meant tons of sugar and maybe some cream.

But she could tell that Rock was almost as done with dinner as she was. Done with the people, not the food.

Cora was sweet as always and she'd done her part to include Pilar and Rock in the conversation as much as she could, but her father was acting like he turned to stone whenever Rock spoke. And as much as everyone tried to smooth it over it was really getting to Kate. The first time she'd ever brought someone to a family dinner, and he was getting the cold shoulder from her father.

Her flesh and blood.

Cora was a doll, as always. And as frustrating as Walker was, Kate knew that the emotional parts of Roan and Walker's personality were equal parts of their father and their mother. They were both really good guys at their core.

And her dad, her only blood relative at the table was acting like a total ass.

Sitting between Kate and Roan, Pilar was trying to find a way to bridge the gap. Kate could read her good intentions on the other woman's face. She only wished that she could tell Pilar that it was okay, not to bother, but the fact that Pilar was trying so much more than her own father drove home how sad and disappointing the situation was.

"Have you given thoughts to when and where you'll have the ceremony?"

Cora's question was to be expected. She'd practically

asked it in every round of texts to Roan and maybe a few emails.

Kate saw Pilar ease into the answer as Roan covered her hand with his.

"There are a number of beautiful gardens in and around Center City. We think it would be a good idea to shoot for the later part of Spring. I have to plan with enough time to get my family to come up from San Antonio."

Roan looked like he was dazzled by his fiancé, just like he should be. "I can't wait to see you surrounded by flowers."

They shared a look that almost turned up the heat in the room before Walker stepped in to add a little bit of information. "Pilar's brother is going to be the one with the hardest time scheduling. He's a Special Agent with the FBI."

Cora nodded. "Goodness! That's a mighty tough job. So much responsibility."

Charles managed a half-shrug. "What about you?" Her father didn't even bother with Rock's name. "You have a good job with the firefighters?"

"I can show you an article from the local paper," Pilar grinned at Rock before she looked back at the Turners. "Rock saved the life of an elderly woman from a fire recently. It was a really touching story and they didn't cover it in the papers, but he took flowers to her and a bunch of us went to the funeral for her sister who died."

Kate smoothed her hand up his forearm and gave Rock a gentle squeeze. "You're one of the best men I've ever known."

His eyes darkened even as his expression lightened. This man... she wanted to be worthy of him. She wanted that so much.

"Roan saves lives every day. Still haven't seen a news article about that. Interesting what stories they chose to magnify, hmm?"

And there it went.

Her last fuck.

Kate stood straight up, and Rock settled her chair as he got to his feet in a reflexive movement. The brothers did the same, but Charles sat ramrod straight in his seat.

"Dad. I'd like to talk to you please."

Charles turned a worried look to his wife before looking up in the vicinity of Kate's face. "We can talk later, Kate. Why don't you sit down, and we can finish dinner."

Kate took a step to the side and then backed away from her chair. "I'm done with dinner, Dad. So, either you can come with me so we can talk, or I can just walk out of the whole restaurant and go home.

With a curious look, Charles Turner got to his feet and dropped his napkin down on the once pristine tablecloth. "Okay. Let's talk."

Cora touched his arm before he rounded the table and he bent down to her so she could say something. Kate leaned against Rock and reveled in the feeling of his hard chest under her fingers. She smiled up at Rock and tried to put him at ease even if she wasn't sure she could manage the same. "Don't worry. I promise not to shoot him."

Rock lifted a brow at that. "You don't have your handgun with you."

Her smile was so sweet it almost terrified him. "I don't have my service weapon." She lifted her clutch from the table and held it up before him.

She knew that later he'd want to get a look at what she was carrying.

Kate knew she'd let him. Especially if he let her search him for... other things.

And that thought alone kept her sanity together as her father followed her out onto the balcony through the side door.

Gabrielle's stood in the center of conservation land that was given to Center City by the estate of Alexander Dunne. His house, a late Georgian Style mansion had been converted into a museum and restaurant. From the balcony, even in the moonlight, a person could see acres and acres of natural landscape features and curated gardens.

In a perfect world, Kate imagined that she might have come out here with Rock to enjoy the quiet, but her life wasn't perfect. Neither was her family.

Everyone could make mistakes. Goodness knows she had issues sometimes with the tone of her voice or the times she'd said things that had been taken badly by others. Still, she tried. Tried to do her best and offer apologies when she was wrong.

"What's your problem, dad?"

"Well, nice to see you too."

She shook her head. "Don't try guilt with me. If you wanted a nicer greeting, you could have gotten one. You've been cold and standoffish all night and I'm tired of waiting for you to reach out to me or even try to make a connection."

"Connection?" He shook his head. "Why didn't you tell us you were bringing someone to dinner?"

"Tell you? Cora already told me to bring someone. Why did I have to tell you I was? What purpose would that have served? Maybe you wanted to dig around and find out something to complain about? Well, let me tell you about the man you're pissing off in there."

HER ROCK

He shook his head and grumbled. "Pissing off? What kind of a man is that?"

"He's not pissed off about how you're treating him, dad. He's pissed off for me. He knows how stressed out I've been about this dinner. He knows how strange our relationship is and he doesn't like it, dad. He doesn't like the way you ignore me. The way you don't connect with me."

She drew in a deep breath and then slowly let it out.

"It's one thing for you to be all about the boys. Walker and Roan are awesome! We all take care each other. We root for each other.

"They know Rock and they know what he means to me. What I mean to him. And they've seen the way Rock stands by me when I need support and the way he cares for me when I need him. But only Rock knows how I've been walking on pins and needles waiting to see you and your reaction to him."

Her dad tilted his head to the side and shook his head. "You mean that you want me to tell you that dating an older man is okay? It's a waste of time, Kate. You're not young anymore. What do you think is going to happen when you have children? How is he going to help you with them when he should be retiring?"

She could only stare at him for a long moment.

"You bastard."

He seemed completely shocked by her outburst. But she was only getting started.

"You want to bring age into this? You have no idea about him or about me when it comes to that."

Her father scoffed at the idea. "I know your age! I've worried about you finding someone to settle down with for more than a decade. So, this is not the time to fool around with a guy just because he's got muscles. Don't settle for sexual attraction. I've done plenty of that myself."

"Wow," she stared at him, "thanks for that self-own, dad."

He lifted a hand and leaned his forehead heavily into his palm. "I don't know what the hell that means. But what I know is that just being attracted to someone doesn't guarantee that you'll be happy with them."

"Like you and mom. You were happy once. I remember that. I remember road trips and fun times at the beach-"

"That was what we tried to give you, Kate, but even from the first, your mother and I struggled to have a relationship beyond sex. We had you and that was great, but we started to grow further and further apart, and I had issues at work."

Kate folded her arms across her chest. "You mean you went through a string of secretaries because you couldn't keep your dick in your pants?"

He shook his head. "There's no need to be crass, Kate."

"I'm a woman working in a traditional man's world. Deal with it, dad."

"I just don't want you to make the same mistakes that I made along the way. Until I met Cora, I had no idea what it meant to love someone more than myself."

His words and his clear honesty hit Kate like a wall of bricks. He hadn't even touched her, and she felt bruised and bloodied.

"Don't worry, dad. I get what you're saying. I do. And I've made peace with all of the crap you did to me and my mother. I know what I'm fighting against inside of me. I know where I can improve and I'm working on it."

She heard the balcony door open slowly and she saw Rock standing in the doorway, watching her with all the love he felt shining in his eyes. She knew she didn't deserve him, but she was going to do her best to change that.

She gave her father one last look and a little piece of her mind. "For a long time, I refused to fall in love because for some reason I had a really warped sense of what it was because of what I saw between you and mother. That's all changed now.

"I see love in all of its forms. All of its glory. And while I'm sure I'm going to make a hellish number of mistakes; I'm never going to shy away from it anymore. When I love, I'm going to grab on with both hands and do whatever it takes to make it work.

"And I need you to understand that Rock is it for me. So, if you can't treat him like a worthy part of his family then please don't expect me to be around you ever again."

She saw him draw back as if he'd been slapped.

"That's a lot to ask of me, Kate. I don't know if I can agree to all of that."

She blinked back the tears threatening to fall and gave him a nod. "When they say opposites attract, they weren't kidding. Cora is all about love and family. You're not. I just hope you don't throw away this relationship down the line. And look, I'll be here in Center City. If you decide to change your ways and become an honest to god, caring person. You know where to find me. Until then, don't... just don't."

She turned away and walked toward the balcony door. A huge weight was lifted from her shoulders and her stomach wasn't twisted up in her belly anymore.

Kate stepped into Rock's arms just inside the door and she leaned into his chest, listening to the powerful rhythm of his heart.

"I'm with you, you know?"

He hugged her closer. "I'm a damn lucky man to have you."

"And I can't believe I was stupid enough to keep you at arm's length for so long."

Rock rubbed his cheek against hers and sent tingles all over her body. "We've been closer than that on a number of occasions."

"I was thinking..."

"Uh oh."

She pinched his side and listened to him beg her to stop, laughing while he did it. "I was thinking I want dessert after all."

He grinned down at her. "What do you want to order?"

Kate looked at the incredibly amazing man standing beside her and smiled. "You. Let's go back to your place."

"Yes, ma'am. Anything you say, ma'am."

She poked him in the side as they started walking toward the front door. "I love you, Martin Ferris. Thank you for being my rock."

"Always," he wrapped his arm around her shoulder and pulled her into an alcove for a kiss, "always."

NEXT... THE MAN FOR HER

Next in the series will be the story of Theo Noble & Irish Healey
 The Man For Her

ACKNOWLEDGMENTS

Thanks so much to all of the readers!!

Lots of cyber hugs and kisses to my Alpha, Beta, and Gamma ladies who keep me going along the way - Thuy P, Kathy L, & Rachael B! You ladies are like caffeine in all the best ways.

And for this particular book - Thanks to two special readers who helped name characters in Center City -

TV Reporter Kennedy Heart was named by Lisa Role Courter

And Civil Lawyer Serena Campos was named by Lily Kwan

I'm so grateful for their help!

ABOUT THE AUTHOR

Books have always been a big part of my life. Reading was an escape from my classmates who teased me because of my speech impediment. Books were the walls of my castle, protecting my fortress, and allowed me to bask in the sunlight of my beautiful labyrinth filled with fantasies.

Now, I hope that I can share that same gift with others. If I can give them a place of shelter, of joy, and yes... love, then I will count myself blessed.

OTHER BOOKS BY REINA TORRES

Reina writes a variety of romance books from Heat to Sweet and back again...

Most of Reina's books are available in KINDLE UNLIMITED

First Responders

San Antonio First Responders Series

Justice for Sloane

When Sloane's life is in danger, FBI Agent Vicente Bravo steps in to make sure she's safe, but his heart isn't safe from falling in love.

Justice for Miranda

Retired Game Warden Miranda finds herself in the crosshairs of a drug smuggler. Her former partner, Trace Carson, is ready to protect her, but is he ready for love?

Shelter for Viviana

Station Seven Fire Chief, Ethan Blaise, has seen an entire shift of his firefighters find love. At a wedding, the caterer catches his eye and soon, he and Viviana Martenz are heating up more than her kitchen.

Justice for Hildie

Hildie Faraday helps women and children in need. Nothing will stop her, even a man with a gun and an axe to grind with her. Texas Ranger Jake McGowan is going to do everything he can to protect her, because it's more than his job, he's in love with the stubborn, hard-headed woman.

Justice for Blyss

Being a Texas Game Warden was always Blyss Hardy's dream. Helping to protect wildlife and nature of her home state is exciting, unless it involves Owen Mercier, the hotter than hell retile wrangler who is determined to make her... his.

Shelter for Aylin

Aylin Blaise, daughter of Station Seven's Fire Chief, is loving her life. Well, most of it. An extended family of first responders and friends in college are expanding her world in leaps and bounds, but the one person she really wants to spend more time with, is keeping his distance. Will Stillman realize his mistake in time?

Military Romance

Delta Force Hawaii Series

Rescuing Hi'ilani

Jackson "Ajax" Guard made a mistake giving up the woman he loved when he joined the Delta Force – Now he has a second chance to love her, but he needs to keep her alive first.

A Hero for Ku'uipo

Ephrain "Train" Figueroa can't believe his luck when his Delta Force Unit travels to the island of Kaua'i for training and he meets Ku'uipo Ornellas, a woman who becomes more than his sweetheart... she's the one he's been looking for all of his life.

Single Title –

The Mechanic

Adam Masterson didn't know what hit him when the most beautiful woman's car broke down in his parking lot. Blake Lennox had never realized how heavy the world felt sitting on her shoulders until Adam helped lift it... with his arms around her.

Shifter Romance that will bring the Heat

Mystic Mountain Series – a Mountain Resort where Shifters are at home

Winter

He's waited for years to claim his mate. Now there's no holding back.

Xavier

He valued his solitude and freedom, until he met her.

Locke

He felt the weight of the world on his shoulders. She gave him back his fire.

The Orsino Security Series – Three Bears who find their fated mates (BBW)

Her UnBearable Protector

He may be the one hired to protect her, but she brought him to life.

His UnBearable Touch

Her music calmed the beast within him and he brought light into her darkness.

Their UnBearable Destiny

He may be the youngest, but he's no baby bear, and she'll make him earn his place at her side… and love every minute of the chase.

Sylvan City Alphas –

The Tiger's Innocent Bride

When his mate's life is in danger, Devlin has to make the choice between keeping his animal a secret or saving her life. To him there's sonly one choice. Love.

Too Much To Bear

A single dad to a whole house of foster shifters, Boone asks for help from a Dating Agency to find his mate. How could he know that the first try would be the only one he'd need?

The Fighter

When Cage has a hard time understanding how to keep his teenage foster's moods and asks for help. Who knew that the answer to his trouble was also the missing piece of his soul?

Bear His Mark

He's looking for a mate to have and hold and she's afraid she's full of broken pieces. These two opposites might just make the perfect whole.

Small Town Contemporary Romance with Heat –

St. Raphael, CA Series –

Finding Home

Neither of them wanted to find love when they moved to St. Raphael. Fate & his Nonna had other plans.

Playing With Fire

She swore off 'True Love' – He wants 'Happy Ever After.' How could this end badly?

Healing Hearts

They're both going after their dreams. Little did they know that they'd find love along the way, with each other.

Taking A Chance

They dedicated years of their lives to their careers. When they met, they decided to take a chance on love.

Sweet Holiday Romance Contemporary

A Dance for Christmas

His daughter's favorite dance teacher agrees to join them as part of their family on stage in the Nutcracker. What a perfect Christmas miracle to fall in love and make their family real!

Sweet Western Historical Romance –

Bower, Colorado Series –

Home to Roost

He wasn't looking for love, so he wasn't expecting the perfect woman to stumble across his path.

Imogene's Ingenuity

She came to Bower hoping to work in the print shop and ends up falling for the printer

Three Rivers Express Series –

Always, Ransom (Book 1)

He rode for the Pony Express through a score of dangers on the trail. Danger followed her to her doorstep. Would their love end before it even began?

Always, Wyeth (Book 3)

Tillie lived a life driven by her father's ambition, when she met Wyeth she found joy and love. Will her father allow her to be happy?

Always, Ellis (Book 5)

Ellis spent years in prison for trusting the wrong people, but when he meets the Marshal's daughter he finds himself working harder than ever for redemption… and love

Ellingsford, Montana Series-

Stay With Me

In a world trying to bend their wills, these two lonely souls will find their strength together.

Her Gentle Heart

A man who never asked for help, a woman who gave him what he needed, Her Gentle Heart.

Hold Her Close

A world-weary gambler meets a young woman trying to keep her family together. Is he ready to make a bet on love?

Stand Alone-

The Sailor & The Siren

He found a job on a paddlewheel boat and fell in love with a young woman whose voice and beautiful soul was the melody his heart was searching for.

Printed in Great Britain
by Amazon